Losing Hit Points

Losing Hit Points

KRISTOPHER MIELKE

JAMES LORIMER & COMPANY LTD., PUBLISHERS
TORONTO

For Miranda, whose Help actions always let me roll with advantage.

James Lorimer & Company Ltd., Publishers acknowledges funding support from the Ontario Arts Council (OAC), an agency of the Government of Ontario. We acknowledge the support of the Canada Council for the Arts. This project has been made possible in part by the Government of Canada and with the support of Ontario Creates.

Canada | Canada Council for the Arts Conseil des arts du Canada | ONTARIO ARTS COUNCIL CONSEIL DES ARTS DE L'ONTARIO an Ontario government agency un organisme du gouvernement de l'Ontario | ONTARIO CREATES | Ontario

Cover design: Tyler Cleroux
Cover image: Kate Phillips

Library and Archives Canada Cataloguing in Publication

Title: Losing hit points / Kristopher Mielke.
Names: Mielke, Kristopher, author.
Series: RealLove.
Description: Series statement: Real love
Identifiers: Canadiana (print) 20230535577 | Canadiana (ebook) 20230535585 | ISBN 9781459418097 (hardcover) | ISBN 9781459418080 (softcover) | ISBN 9781459418103 (EPUB)
Subjects: LCGFT: Romance fiction. | LCGFT: Novels.
Classification: LCC PS8626.I355 L67 2024 | DDC jC813/.6—dc23

Published by:
James Lorimer & Company Ltd., Publishers
117 Peter Street, Suite 304
Toronto, ON, Canada
M5V 0M3
www.lorimer.ca

Distributed in Canada by:
Formac Lorimer Books
5502 Atlantic Street
Halifax, NS, Canada
B3H 1G4
www.formaclorimerbooks.ca

Distributed in the US by:
Lerner Publisher Services
241 1st Ave. N.
Minneapolis, MN, USA
55401
www.lernerbooks.com

Printed and bound in Canada.

NOTE FROM THE SCRIBE

When I decided I wanted to write a book about queer teens playing D&D, *I didn't know nearly enough about how to actually play* Dungeons & Dragons. *I'd only ever played a few times, so I borrowed several pounds of books from friends. I listened to podcasts and watched actual-plays on YouTube. I got really into* Critical Role, Dimension 20, *and* Not Another D&D Podcast.

Despite all my research, I'm still not an expert. But the most important thing I realized was that I don't have to be. And to read this book, or to actually play D&D, *you don't have to be either. As Brian Murphy says, "if you've listened to a* D20 *campaign, you've already absorbed enough knowledge to start your own campaign. So what if you have to look up the rules sometimes?" That doesn't seem so intimidating to me anymore.*

If you're not already a D&D *player, I hope* Losing Hit Points *gives you enough inspiration to start playing. Maybe you even want to borrow a few characters or locations. At the back of this book, you can find the character sheets and location notes I used to write Journey and Rumour's tabletop adventure. Go forth, brave adventurers, and have fun.*

– K. A. Mielke, 2023

01 An Elf Walks into a Café

I'M FINISHING THE NEW ISSUE of *Daredevil* when my cousin, Hamish, spills coffee on his shirt. For, like, the tenth time.

"Why does Clive let you drink anything but water?" I say, scooching the comic away from the dots of whipped cream on the counter. "You're cursed."

Hamish brushes his fingers over the brown stains on his shirt. A white, short-sleeved button-up with a cacti pattern. It was a nice shirt this morning. "Clive lets me do whatever I want because I'm the best at upselling."

"Because you do nothing but read comics."

"I'm sorry, Journey, is reading comics not cool? Are you not reading a comic as we speak? Did you not beg me to get you a job in a comic store?"

I did literally beg Hamish for this job. And when he said no, because it's a small place, because there are fewer than five employees, because Clive wouldn't appreciate Hamish asking for a favour, I used my special move: I told our moms.

Not my proudest moment, but I can't deny the results.

More than a comic shop, more than a board game café, Limited Series is a one-stop shop for nerd stuff. The kind of place I dreamed of as a kid, full of toys, comics, board games, and t-shirts.

This is actually where I bought the hat I'm wearing, a red *King of Coats* toque with the series' iconic Cufflinks of Clarity, four small silver diamonds that form one big diamond. *King of Coats* is a part of my DNA. An instant nostalgia switch on my heart.

And probably the reason I'm a big nerd working at a comic book store.

We're in the South End, far from the foot traffic of downtown and not near enough to the University of Guelph campuses to ever really be busy. The only customers here are Greta and Nathan, Hamish's long-time friends and roommates, sitting in the dining area and waiting for *D&D* to start.

"How many paperback sales turned hardcover sales do I need to be as great as you, O Mighty Hamish?" I say, as Hamish dabs his shirt with a crumpled ball of napkins.

"You simply could never. There is no other quite like me."

"Yeah, that checks out."

Hamish takes another sip of what must be his fifth latte. More coffee spills down his chin, dripping from his ginger beard onto his round belly. He drinks more coffee when he's anxious, which only makes him more anxious, and I'll bet money this isn't his last latte of the night.

I set the issue of *Daredevil* back on the top of my To Be Read pile. I'll have to find out how Matt Murdock and Elektra mess up their relationship yet again when I'm out of the splash zone.

"Do you need a bib?" I ask.

"I'd wear a bib and make it look so cool, don't you test me."

I believe it. There's a style element to being publicly queer that I, non-binary and bisexual though I am, just don't understand. I dress like every straight boy nerd I know in my graphic tees and jeans. But I'm trying to be less basic with my open navy waistcoat.

Baby steps.

Hamish, on the other hand, pulls together the most fashionable outfits with half-off thrift store finds, even though when I go to the thrift store I only find t-shirts with wine mom slogans and pants that don't fit. He's like an alchemist turning lead into gold, except the alchemy is his natural confidence.

Even at four years old, Hamish refused to wear dresses. He told his parents, teachers, and bullies that he was a boy and would be treated as such. That's how confident he's always been about who he is and what he wants. It shows in everything he does.

Which makes it weird how nervous he is about tonight.

"You're gonna do great," I tell him.

"You don't know Nathan like I do," Hamish says, stubby fingers raking through his blue undercut. "I let him beta read a short story for me once and he tore it to shreds — literally, he printed it off himself and ripped it up in front of me, he hated it so much. I've never met a harsher critic. Offline, anyway."

"I'll be here to back you up."

"Please, you couldn't back up a car with a rear camera. You're a wallflower. I'm doomed."

The front door opens and an elf child enters Limited Series — I mean, a child dressed as an elf. Melting snow flattens their long black hair, dripping from the curls framing their chubby cheeks. They bump into the life-sized cutout of Tom Holland as Spider-Man and apologize to him as they prop him back up. Their long green cloak brushes the snowy heels of their boots, soaking the hem. Dark brown ears match their skin tone but not their proportions, sticking out in a way that makes them look like one of those cute little desert foxes.

They look kind of familiar.

"Hi there!" Hamish calls, setting aside his napkins. "How can we help you today?"

"Um, hi." The kid looks at their boots, their fingers playing with a loose thread dangling from their cloak. "I'm here for, um, *Dungeons & Dragons* night? Is that . . . a thing?"

"Another party member! That sure is a thing, a thing that starts in fifteen minutes. We'll be setting up at that big table over there if you want to sit."

"I just need to wait for my sister. She's — oh, there she is! Rumour, come on!"

My heart skips a beat. I do know this kid. I've known him and his sister most of my life.

In walks my ex-best friend, Rumour Gatwa.

02 The Psychic Damage of Pure Awkwardness

SEEING AN OLD FRIEND shouldn't make me struggle to breathe. Or make my heart pound like I'm running a marathon. But it does.

She does.

Rumour's long black hair flows from the top of her high ponytail. Gelled edges curl in semi-circles on either side of her forehead. Snowflakes melt on her warm brown skin, beads of water rolling down her cheek. She's wearing long press-on nails, the same hot pink as her shirt and her puffy winter coat.

For a long moment, Rumour takes in the store. Her gaze flicks from the giant stuffed spider, Shelob, hanging in the corner of the entryway to the seven orange Dragon Balls dangling by fishing line over my head. She stops at our stuffie collection of Sonic the Hedgehogs, *Stardew Valley* Junimos, and *Dragon Quest* Slimes.

Her wide-set amber-brown eyes glitter in their pools of pink eyeshadow. She looks like a sailor stumbling upon the Fountain of Youth.

I know that look. I'd worn that look. Limited Series really is Nerd Heaven.

But then her gaze settles on the cash register. On me behind it. And I guess Limited Series might actually be Nerd Hell, depending on how the next couple hours go.

I grab *Daredevil* like a lifeline. Should I hold it in front of my face and pretend I don't know her? That I'm not even here? I'm already rolling ones in both Charisma and Stealth, not to mention Acting Like a Functioning Human Being. I don't know what to do with my hands. Breathing feels weird and I can't stop thinking about it, which only makes it feel *weirder* —

"Hey," Hamish says. "You joining us for *D&D*?"

"Under duress," Rumour says.

Out of the corner of my eye, I can tell she's looking at me. I don't return the eye contact. My fingers dig noisily through the box of open fidget toys on the counter, something I regret doing immediately on account of the noise. But now I have to grab a fidget because not grabbing one would be so weird!

"I don't know what 'duress' means," says her little brother, Ian, "but I'm pretending it means 'heck yes and I'll love it!'"

"*D&D* isn't as scary as it seems," Hamish says. "There's a little improv acting, a little random chance, and a little math — but mostly it's just us, hanging out and telling a story together."

I flick a *Legend of Zelda* Hylian shield fidget spinner. I don't know how much she's changed, but the Rumour I knew loved telling stories. I just don't think telling stories with me is a great selling point.

But she says, "Might as well. I did spend an hour making a character."

"That's the spirit," Hamish says. "I was just telling our young elf here that we'll get started in a few, right around the corner. Can we get you anything to snack on while you wait? You could even roll a d20 and let fate decide."

Hamish slides a laminated menu and a blue, gem-like d20 toward them.

"I don't know if I trust my luck," Rumour says, as Ian snatches up the menu.

"Fair enough," Hamish says. "A critical miss is Halloween candy from who-knows-when, so . . ."

Scanning the pun-filled menu, Ian's eyes light up. He holds it in front of his sister. "What's a Solid Milk . . . snake?"

"It's a *Metal Gear* joke," I mumble, flicking the shield.

"And an actual milkshake," Hamish says.

"It's a stretch," Rumour says.

"Stretching wordplay is part of our charm,"

Hamish counters. "No snakes were harmed in its making, though it is nearly solid."

"I want one!" Ian says. "Can I get one?"

Hamish waggles his blue eyebrows. "See? The charm must be working."

"All right, one of those for him," Rumour says. "And I'll have a . . . Hastega, please."

"Legally I need to warn you, that has three shots of espresso."

"Really?" Ian asks.

"No to the legality," Hamish says. "Yes to the caffeine."

Rumour slides twenty bucks across the counter. "I'll need it if I'm going to brave the fast-paced world of tabletop roleplaying."

"We're not that scary once you get to know us." Hamish pops open the cash register. He passes back Rumour's change and also a palm-sized *Mario* coin block.

"Mine!" Ian says, snatching the block.

"Watch it with those grabby hands," Rumour says.

"Put that on your table so we know where to bring the drinks," Hamish says, even though the café is basically empty. "See you out there."

Rumour thanks him, pockets the change, and turns to find Ian at the circular t-shirt rack.

With Rumour out of my hit box, I can breathe again. But my stomach squirms. Now I have to roleplay with Rumour all evening, trying not to make an ass of myself.

If it's not too late, considering I already pretended I was invisible.

Hands busy with the rumbling espresso machine, Hamish nudges me with his shoe. "Why does she look familiar? And why are you acting so weird?"

Shit. Hamish noticed. That means it's *way* too late.

"We used to be friends," I say. "Like, best friends. Used to hang out all the time."

The words don't begin to explain what Rumour was to me. What she still is, even if it's complicated and one-sided. You can't scoop a single bucket out of the ocean and expect to understand its true depth. All the life thriving where the sunlight can't reach.

I sigh. "You know her."

"I babysat you all the time and I don't remember her." The machine spurts a noisy burst of steam. "Didn't you only have, like, one friend?"

"Same friend. Rumour looked pretty different before she transitioned."

"One of us, one of us," Hamish chants.

Her brother looked different too. Ian used to be the cutest six-year-old in the entire world. But time stops for no ex-friends. Now he's almost doubled in size, ten years old, and showing up at my work in a cloak and elf ears.

"And, if I'm not mistaken, you *like* like her," Hamish adds, like a middle schooler.

"How dare you," I say.

"Not a strong denial, my friend."

"Doesn't matter. There's a good reason we're not friends anymore." In my chest, a knife of a memory twists. Guilt flows like blood from the emotional wound. "You better not make it weird."

"I don't think you need my help making it weird."

"Not much of a promise."

Hamish busies himself with the milkshake, grinning like a trickster god. I don't trust him not to get me into trouble with frost giants in an attempt to be my wingman.

Across the shop, Rumour gets down on one knee, at eye level with Ian. Ian's face has fallen, the excitement turning into nervousness or fear. He's balled up his cloak, holding it in front of his chest and tugging at its threads as he stares into the tabletop gaming room.

I remember the three of us roleplaying at the park in a thunderstorm, the summer before grade nine. One of the last times. I'm swinging a stick as long as my body, my imagination transforming it into the biggest, coolest anime sword. Rumour's standing up to her shins in a puddle, her stick held in the air like a staff — like she's causing the flashes of lightning in the sky. Ian's hanging from the climber, its metal support beams the legs of a monster, its slide a child-snatching trunk, and he's crying for help because he's about to be eaten.

My clothes are soaked and I'm happy, *so* happy.

Sure, it wasn't our safest roleplay session, but we played *King of Coats* all the time back then, in all weather. It felt like Ian was my brother, too.

Rumour speaks too quietly for me to hear. She points to the tabletop room. Then she points to the parking lot. Options.

They might leave. And if Rumour leaves now, she might never come back.

My heart somersaults. I know I was a jerk — in the past and also five minutes ago. Maybe my awkwardness gets a buff around Rumour and I failed my first saving throw. That doesn't mean I can't do better. Make it right.

I toss the fidget spinner back in the box, close *Daredevil*, and step around the counter. I'm at the t-shirt rack before I have a plan. They both turn to face me. Tears swim in Ian's eyes.

I grab a *Stranger Things* t-shirt and move it to the right with a loud screech of the metal coat hanger.

"Um," I say. "Hey."

"Oh, so you do see us," Rumour snaps. Not holding back at all.

It's a critical hit.

"I — I'm just —" *I didn't want to make you uncomfortable. I'm sorry.* "I was really into the comic I was reading."

"Sure," she says without feeling.

"Is everything okay?"

"We're fine."

"I'm . . . I'm kinda scared," Ian says, cloak wrapped around his knuckles. "I've never actually played *D&D* before."

Rumour looks at Ian like he's giving a robo-call too much personal information, but I kneel beside her. "This will be my first time, too. I watch a lot of *Critical Role* and *Dimension 20*, but I'm nervous about actually saying things. *Out loud.* Maybe we can help each other out."

"How?" Ian asks.

"We'll be a team. If any of the trolls, in-game or around the table, try us, we'll have each other's back. What do you think?"

The grip on his cloak loosens. I can make out the points of the coin block wrapped inside the fabric. Even Rumour's glare softens — until she catches me looking at her and raises her shield once more.

"Okay," Ian says. "We can try."

At that, Hamish's Midwestern emo playlist cuts off. The nasally sung poetry about punching your dad is replaced by a gentle, 8-bit JRPG melody. The opening track to one of the earlier *Final Fantasy* games.

Hamish drums his hands on the counter. "All righty, folks. Who's ready for adventure?"

03 The Fellowship of the Coffee Table Rings

"I'M JUST SAYING," Nathan says, "the new *King of Coats* show is pandering."

At six-foot-five, Nathan towers over the curvy, South Korean woman beside him, his girlfriend Greta. He's a thin, pale, hairy man, like the skeleton of Rasputin with his hair intact. Trading robes for a brick red cardigan and khaki slacks.

"So what?" Greta asks, her mouth full of tortilla chip and "N7 layer dip." She sports a naturally grey buzz cut despite only being in her early twenties. Every single time I've seen Greta she's worn a different homemade item of clothing. Today, it's a simple sleeveless dress with a pattern of cartoon bombs, their wicks sparking.

"So that's what makes it crap!"

She points a chip at him. "You barely watched five minutes."

The big, round table is already set up. In the centre of the table is grid paper with a blueprint drawn on it in Sharpie and a handful of mini-figures in a pile. In front of Nathan and Greta are their notebooks, bags of dice, character sheets, and Nathan's own copy of the *5th Edition D&D Player's Handbook.*

Greta's character sheet has salsa or, as the menu puts it, "Krogan Blood," splashed dangerously close to the doodle of a half-orc in glasses. A tangled lump of yarn sits on Greta's left, knitting needles jammed inside.

Hamish takes his seat behind a cardboard divider with a big scene of fantasy art, dragons and goblins and warriors doing battle. Rumour and Ian sit between Greta and Hamish. I sit beside Nathan.

The couple continues arguing like we're not here.

"Every show panders," Greta says. "Every piece of media *ever* plays to its audience. The original *King of Coats* trilogy pandered — you're just grumpy the new direction isn't pandering to you anymore."

"Whatever," Nathan says. "You're ignoring what pandering means."

"Or maybe you're focusing too hard on what yelly YouTube boys tell you pandering means."

Hamish loudly clears his throat. "Newcomers, meet Greta and Nathan. They do love each other, I promise."

Greta takes a deep breath, turns to the Gatwas beside her, and smiles. "Hi, I'm Greta! My pronouns are she and her. The grumpy Sasquatch is Nathan. His pronouns are he and him."

Nathan grunts. Rumour shares her pronouns (she/her) and Ian shares his (he/him). They already know me, they/them enby that I am, so I just give Greta a small wave.

"Journey-not-the-Destination," Greta says, "how did your essay go?"

"You were right," I say. "Once I started thinking

of it like an anime, *The Great Gatsby* was way more interesting."

Rumour snorts, covering her mouth. My cheeks feel like a homemade fire starter, dryer lint in a toilet paper tube. All it takes to light me up is a single positive emotion.

My heart clings to her laughter, waiting for a sign that there will be more snorts at my expense. But my mind knows this is desperate weirdo behaviour and runs the other way. I can't meet her eyes.

"Speaking of *King of Coats*," Hamish says, even though the conversation has moved on, "I remember a couple of rascals who used to roleplay Zephyr Morningblade and Princess Cassandra at Exhibition Park. Swinging sticks like swords, casting pretend fireballs, and wearing their moms' bathrobes as the magical coats."

Hamish rests his chin on steepled fingers, menacing from behind his partition.

I feel like I should be throwing a d20 for a Constitution check. I give Hamish my best "please shut up" look, because I knew he would do this! Like I said, trickster god. Cosmic shit disturber.

"Are you going anywhere with that sentence?" Nathan says.

"He's talking about me and Journey," Rumour says. She can definitely tell what Hamish is up to, trying to be the all-powerful Dungeon Master of our actual lives. "When we were dumb kids doing dumb kid things."

Like hanging out at all. Like trusting each other.

"Hey, what's wrong with roleplaying in the park?" Ian says. "My friends and I do it all the time."

"Sorry, lil dude," Rumour says, bringing Ian in by the shoulders and kissing his temple. He wriggles out of her grip like he's embarrassed in front of his cool new friends. "But we were particularly dumb kids."

"I can't argue with the facts," I say.

"You literally ate dirt — and I quote — 'for the authenticity,'" she says.

"I had a vocabulary instead of common sense. And it was magic dirt."

Rumour gives me a tight smile. Then she turns to Greta, moving on before we're trapped in this painful limbo forever. "I love your dress."

"Thanks." Greta winks. "It's *the bomb.*"

Nathan rolls his eyes. "The only reason she chose that fabric was so she could make that joke."

"One might say I'm pandering to my pun-loving audience."

"Oh my god."

"Hamish is a writer," Greta says, "let's ask him."

"Don't you have to make money writing to be a writer?" Nathan says.

"How about we leave Hamish completely out of it," Hamish says. "I already deal with every argument at home. Tonight, I'm not your friend. I am your Dungeon Master."

Tonight is Hamish's first night as Dungeon Master. He's spent weeks working on this campaign. Years, actually, considering it's based on the novels he's been sending to literary agents. Novels that have gotten him, like, a hundred rejections.

He's being really vulnerable by turning his precious work into a campaign. One in which players can mess up and make fun of whatever they want right to his face.

I take the square of my character sheet from my pocket and unfold it. From my other pocket, I pull out the small handful of dice Hamish loaned me, black with orange and red flames like a Guy Fieri shirt, each a different shape because each has a different number of sides. "Adventure time is wasting, DM."

"Quite right," Hamish says. "Did anyone need any last minute help with their character sheets?"

"I, um, I actually have a couple questions," Ian says. "There are, like, a lot of numbers. I guess I just want to know what . . . they're . . . for?"

He visibly cringes at himself. Nathan makes a face.

I jump in before Ian is made to feel any worse. "It can't hurt to give a rundown of the basic mechanics," I say.

"For sure, for sure," Hamish says. "What's about to happen is, I'm your narrator and I'm going to tell a story. You all have your characters, but I will be every other character, every NPC — that's short for Non-Player Character. I'll also tell you information about the world and its people, depending on your interactions with my NPCs and your rolls. Here's where the numbers come in. Your stats give you extra points with certain rolls and checks, or take away points. Let's say I ask for a Strength check. What's your Strength stat?"

"Nine," Ian says.

Hamish looks at his own notes and taps a paper. "The ability modifier of a nine is minus one. So I call for a Strength check. You grab your d20 and roll. You get a six. Six minus one is five. Does that make sense?"

Ian nods. "And what about the other dice?"

"Those will be for attack rolls, depending on your weapon type or your spells. And also sometimes luck rolls. But your d20 is your best friend. You'll use it the most." Hamish smiles and asks Rumour, "How about you? Need any extra help?"

"Picking spells was kind of hard, but I managed," she says. "Like, some were pretty gross. Who would pick Grease?"

"Grease can be useful," Nathan says.

"If you like slapstick comedy, maybe," Rumour says. "And some were weirdly mean. Tasha's Hideous Laughter? What did Tasha do to you, man?"

I laugh. Then I feel like I'm drawing too much attention to myself by laughing, so I sip from my water bottle.

"I had trouble," Greta says. "Nathan watched *very* closely while I rolled my ability scores."

"To protect character sheet integrity!" Nathan says.

"He thinks I'm a cheater," Greta says. "I should have cheated. I didn't roll above a thirteen."

Hamish passes me the cardboard box of miniatures. "Can I get everyone to pick a mini-fig and introduce your characters? Let's start with my beloved deputy."

"Uh, okay." I pick out the only halfling, curly haired and carrying a bow, and set them on the grid paper. I pass the box to Nathan. "I am a halfling fighter named Oakley Goldenrod."

I smooth out the creases of my character sheet. My sketch of Oakley is rough, my lines wobbly. I can still see my half-erased mistakes.

"A halfling *fighter*," Nathan says, unimpressed. He rifles through the miniatures.

"Everyone neglects the kneecaps," I say. "It's an untapped market for small but mighty warriors."

"Sure it is."

Continuing, I say, "Born in the halfling village of Babblinge Brooke, Oakley spent the thirty years of their childhood bored and lonely. Everyone found their daydreaming and their love of adventure stories weird, even their parents, who pressured Oakley to become a baker or a gardener. They left home a year ago looking for adventure. Since then, under the name Oakley the Outstanding, they've travelled the land hunting monsters. For a small fee, of course. But more than money, more than the thrill of the hunt, what Oakley really craves . . . is friendship."

I say the last bit with a dramatic flair and a confidence I don't feel. Once I'm finished, something about my mini-performance makes me tense up. When I used Oakley's pronouns, the same as mine, I avoided even glancing at Rumour.

That . . . really, *really* sucks.

Coming out as non-binary two years ago was

freeing. I'd never been very good at being a boy. I thought *way* more about if I'd been born a girl than is strictly normal for a cisgender boy. But those were never even the only options!

My guilt about how I treated Rumour always cast a shadow over my own journey. I don't know if I'm ready to close the distance between the shadow and its source.

I purse my lips and give Nathan two thumbs-up to let him know it's his turn.

Opening his binder, he flips through a dozen character sheets. "Normally I'd be a bard, but seeing as there is a child present . . ."

"You could try not playing a bard in a gross way?" Greta says.

"What would be the point?"

"I'm a bard!" Ian says, jumping a little in his seat. "I really like your drawings."

"That's because they're good," Nathan says.

Not exactly humble, but he's telling the truth. The art in each of Nathan's draw-your-character-here boxes have crisp, clean lines and full colour. I don't know the first thing about how he gets his colours to pop like that, what markers he uses, or how to even develop those skills.

"I suppose I shall play Ra'ven Tor'el," Nathan says, "pride of the elven woodlands. Orphaned at a young age when goblins murdered his parents, he was raised by his cold and distant lord uncle. What the man lacked in warmth, he made up for in teaching Ra'ven the way of the ranger. At sixteen, he left the elves to rid the world of goblin scum. His purpose in life is to one day find the very goblins who orphaned him."

"Enter Smashwell Stronk!" Greta says, holding up her salsa-stained sheet. Her pencil-drawn, shaded picture of a half-orc looks like one of those old illustrations in *Alice's Adventures in Wonderland* or *Peter Pan*. Smashwell holds a pipe in one giant hand and an open book in the other. "When Smashwell met Ra'ven, she found a kindred spirit. She, too, has left her home in search of a sort of revenge. Growing up a bookworm and a lover of the healing arts among more traditional orcs, she never felt like she belonged anywhere. But then they told her to put down the books and pick up the battle axe, or leave."

"A bookish orc cleric," Nathan says in the same disapproving tone. "This is my own personal ring of hell."

"Times are changing, baby." Greta winks and continues, "So Smashwell left. She met Ra'ven at an independent bookstore, where he was researching to better track his goblin opponents. Smashwell was eager to help, to prove herself in a land where no one respects her raw intellect — yet, that is! While she doesn't agree with Ra'ven's quest to genocide a whole people, I think they make a charming odd couple. Just like real life."

"We love to see it," Hamish says.

"Speak for yourself," Nathan says.

"Is it my turn?" Ian asks.

Hamish says, "It sure is, buddy."

Ian clears his throat, holding his character sheet in front of his face. "Ahem. Um. I . . . am . . . playing . . . a half-elf. And a, uh, a bard. I already said that. His name is Jace. He's one of those guys who, you know, carries a lute everywhere and sings in taverns. He hopes one day he'll be a famous rock star but so far he doesn't make a lot of money. That's it."

"Welcome aboard, the artist known only as Jace," Hamish says.

"Another elf. I see." Nathan flips through his pages again like he's about to change his character, but then he shuts the binder with a grunt. "I usually prefer to be the only member of my race. But this is fine."

"It's 'species' now, babe," Greta says. "Race is so seventies."

Nathan only shakes his head.

"Last but certainly not least," Hamish says, looking at me for a brief but *super* annoying moment, "Rumour. Who will you be playing this evening?"

Rumour sucks her teeth. The hanging café light above our table, in the shape of a d20, makes her glossy lips shine.

I'm staring, which I realize way too late not to feel like a creep. My ears are very warm. I try not to think about how red my face must be.

"Demonica Scribe, tiefling wizard," she says. "As per the guidance of rando tiefling Reddit users, she has an infernal name and a name for a virtuous pursuit. Her past is a mystery to you. Count yourself lucky to be able to witness her future."

"Love the name, love the mystery," Hamish says.

Once every player has a mini-figure on the grid paper, the box of miniatures returns to Hamish.

"Hey, Roo," Ian says, "how old is Demonica?"

"Twenty-four," Rumour says. "Why?"

Grinning, Ian picks up a pencil and crosses something out. He writes something else in its place. "Because I forgot to mention Jace is twenty-five."

"Very funny," she says.

"I know."

"Excuse me, folks." Clive appears in the entryway, slinging a white towel over his shoulder.

He's an older, skinny white man wearing all black. His t-shirt and ball-cap both say LIMITED SERIES in gold font.

"I just wanted to thank you all for coming out,"

he says. "Normally I'm the Dungeon Master, but all masters must eventually take on an apprentice. I trust you'll all treat Hamish with the same respect you'd have treated me."

He smiles specifically at Nathan, who grumbles from the woolly depths of his beard.

"And I would like to remind everyone that I'll be in the kitchen until eleven p.m. Ready and willing to make whatever you need to restore your hit points, recharge your mana, and soothe the soul. Have fun and adventure responsibly!"

"Thank you, Clive!" Greta says, triggering thanks from the rest of us.

Clive retreats to the kitchen.

Hamish taps his phone with a painted black fingernail. The sounds of hushed voices, crackling fire, and clinking glass play from its speakers. Vaguely medieval string music plucks to life.

"We open in a tavern . . ." Hamish says, using the dramatic narrator voice he's been workshopping with me.

"Very original," Nathan says.

"It's a beginner-friendly setting! Besides, you love tropes, Nate. When your faves try to reinvent the wheel, you lose your mind."

"There's a reason wheels are five thousand years old. Wheel round. Round good."

Hamish points at me. "Wallflower."

"Yeah," I say, "sorry."

Ignoring the confusion of everyone else at the table, Hamish continues narrating. "The war of the gods has left the heavens empty . . ."

04 Taverns and Meet-Cutes

THE WAR OF THE GODS *has left the heavens empty, but the world keeps spinning. Life goes on. And patrons arrive at taverns, hungry, thirsty, and looking for work.*

There are many taverns in Pan-Terra, but The Silly Goose has a reputation. In the seaside port city of Crow's Nest, in the kingdom of Reignem, the tavern is simple on the outside. A two-storey building with a thatched roof, the business only recently made enough gold to buy glass for its windows. But its value comes from the adventurers, treasure hunters, and thrill seekers arriving in need of a quest.

Five such adventurers gather at The Silly Goose today, seeking a roof to wait out the storm. They do not know each other but soon, they may have cause to band together . . .

"That's a lot of info-dumping," Nathan says.

"I'm setting the scene," Hamish says.

"It's confusing."

Eyebrows pressed together, Hamish opens his mouth as if to argue. But instead, taking a deep breath, he asks the rest of the group, "Is anyone else confused?"

"I'm sorry, is the town Pan-Terra?" Rumour asks.

"Pantera is a famous groove metal and thrash metal band," Nathan says. "And Spanish for 'panther.'"

"Pan-Terra is the *world*," Hamish says, "'Pan' is Greek for 'all' and 'terra' is Latin for 'earth.'"

"So what's Reignem?" Ian asks.

"The kingdom," Hamish says.

"Not subtle," Nathan mumbles.

"Ah yes, subtlety," Greta says, "the number one concern of people who unironically like *He-Man*."

"Don't you bring the *Masters of the Universe* into this," Nathan says.

"I, for one, would love to hear more about The Silly Goose," I say a bit too loudly.

"Solid effort, J," Hamish says.

"Hey, I'm trying."

The half-orc, Smashwell Stronk, sits at a table near the kitchen. She bites into her third whole roast chicken, tearing steaming meat from its bones. She shares a pint of ale with her frowning elf companion, Ra'ven Tor'el. The pair wait for signs of what brought them here.

Tales of nearby goblin attacks.

In a shadowy corner of the tavern, a tiefling watches the room with yellow eyes. Her hood is unable to cover the spiralling horns on either side of her brow. Well into a difficult life, in a difficult time for tieflings, Demonica Scribe trusts only one person.

By the fireplace, the bard known only as Jace plays his lute to a small audience on ratty sofas. Copper coins are tossed his way. Chump change compared to his big dreams.

And finally, a halfling "monster slayer" tells tales taller than they are to a crowd of amused drunks. No one quite believes the little warrior has exterminated a cave of bugbears or even seen a beholder, but they keep the drinks flowing.

"Pardon me." An older human man in a black robe with red trim rises from his chair. On his table is a single black feather. "I wish to hire a party of adventurers for a simple job. My pockets are deep and my need great. Who among you will aid me?"

"No thanks, mister!" Jace says.

"Oh," Hamish says to Ian. "Are you sure?"

"Yep!"

"Disappointed, the old man waits for a second opinion." Hamish pauses, looking between the rest of us.

I should probably jump in and help. Obviously, Hamish wants us to interact with this Non-Player Character. I even open my mouth to say something. Nothing happens.

Roleplaying is hard, okay?

"The old man returns to his seat," Hamish says, a little like a deflating balloon. "He twirls a black feather between his thumb and forefinger. Judging from his scowl, he looks deeply offended."

"It's too early for a quest," Nathan says. "Are there any signs of goblin activity?"

"Roll an Investigation check."

Nathan grabs his grey metal d20, cups it in both hands, and blows on it. He rolls it on the table with a noisy *clink-clink*.

He growls.

"Nat one already," Greta says, her knitting in her lap. "Get them out now."

"You don't see any goblins," Hamish says. "Nor do you hear anyone talking about goblins. But you can't be sure they're not goblins in disguise. You privately wonder if you might be a goblin, actually."

"That's stupid," Nathan says.

"Take it up with the Dice Gods," Hamish says.

"I still have my ability modifier. Plus one to Intelligence."

"Which is the only reason you aren't lost to the paranoia."

"Who else is in the tavern?" Ian asks. "Who's listening to me — I mean, who's listening to Jace play?"

"A bald gnome sways in their seat, grey brows so thick you can't see their eyes," Hamish says. "Beside them are a pair of teenagers. A dwarf girl with black stubble on her jaw and a muscular human boy. Long blond hair hangs to his hips."

"Big human guy, what's up?" Ian says.

Hamish clears his throat. Pitching his voice deeper and his words slower, he says, "'Uh, hey, man. Love your work.'"

"What can I tell about him?"

"Roll a Perception check and we'll find out."

Ian's hand hovers over his cluster of purple dice. He hesitates.

"Remind me, Dungeon Master," I say before I can think better of it. "Which dice do we use for ability checks?"

For a beat, Hamish blinks at me. I watch so many *D&D* actual-plays, he knows there's no way I'm actually confused. But also because he wants to be the very best DM like no one ever was, he says, "My bad, J. This is one of those times I mentioned earlier, Ian, when your stats give you your ability modifier, and that modifier is added to the number you roll. So you'll roll your d20, and — Ian, what is the Wisdom score on your character sheet?"

"Eleven," Ian says.

"Eleven actually has a modifier of zero, so you don't add anything to your roll."

I nod, tapping my d20 with my index finger. "Cool, cool. Us first-timers will probably keep needing refreshers."

"We do have a lot of newbies here," Hamish agrees. "Don't be afraid to ask questions, everyone."

With more confidence, Ian grabs his d20 and rolls a total of seventeen.

Hamish narrates, "Based on the style of his leather armour and lack of clothing, you think he's a barbarian. You also think he's nervous sitting next to the dwarf girl. Despite needing plenty of leg room, the foot closest to hers is turned at an odd angle as if to avoid getting too close. His eyes keep wandering her way."

I'm suddenly very aware of my feet, toes pointing across from me. Pointing at Rumour. I tuck them behind my chair legs so I don't get into any accidental games of footsies.

"Aww," Ian says. "He's totally got a crush. Can I get him to ask her out? I ask if he comes here lots."

"Give me a Charisma check," Hamish says.

"Easy-peasy, that's my highest stat!"

"I come here often," the young barbarian says. "It's nice to unwind after a long day at the bakery. The family business. I'm technically a certified barbarian, but I came home to help my parents. They actually met at The Silly Goose."

The dwarf girl gives him a shy smile. "That's so sweet."

"Yeah?" The barbarian's cheeks turn red. "I've, um, seen you around."

"Wouldn't you know it," Jace says, strumming his lute, "my music causes true love. Listen to this!"

Fingers flying over the strings of his lute, Jace plays a ballad that makes hearts swell and young single folk really see each other for the first time. His song reaches the peak of emotion when suddenly, the front door blasts off its hinges!

Red-plated creatures scuttle into the tavern. Claws flex at the ends of their arms, one larger than the other. Their long eye stalks wave in the air before training on the kitchen door.

"Oh no," cries the dwarf girl, "it's the Clawbertons!"

"Bring us Chef Laios!" speaks the leader of these crab-men, as lightning flashes behind him. "We have come to take our revenge!"

"Did someone say chef?" Clive asks, popping his head out from the kitchen. "Anyone want anything?"

"No thanks, Clive, we're good!" Hamish shouts over his shoulder. Facing the table, he leans forward with a grin and taps his phone screen. The cozy tavern sounds are replaced by the intensity of *Final Fantasy* battle music. "Roll for initiative."

05 Revenge of the Main Course

"OH, ROLLING FOR INITIATIVE," Hamish explains to Ian and Rumour (and me, technically), "means rolling a d20 to see who goes first in a battle. You also add your Dexterity ability score modifier."

Nathan, Greta, and I all roll our d20s. Hamish rolls for the enemies. Rumour and Ian copy us, tossing their jade green and amethyst purple dice, engraved numbers reflecting golden in the light.

I rolled an eighteen and add my Dex of plus three.

I have to add on my fingers because math is really not my strong suit. That's twenty-one total. We all call out our numbers, except for Nathan.

"Nathan, Nathan, Nathan," Hamish says. "Tell me you didn't."

Nathan holds his head in his hands. Greta rubs his back, a teasing twinkle in her eyes.

"Another nat one," Nathan says.

"At least you have high Dex," Hamish says. "You're not last."

"I'm last in my heart."

"During combat," Hamish says, ignoring him, "one round is about six seconds. You move according to your Speed stat. One square of grid paper takes five movement speed. And you get one action, unless you have any bonus actions. Journey, what'll be the first move?"

"Well, I would have liked a second chance to convince those guys at the bar I was telling the truth," I grumble.

"If the die wills a Charisma fail, a Charisma fail

you shall have. Plus, your Charisma sucks."

"What do I need sweet-talking for? My blade does all the talking for me."

"You could try again," Hamish says, "but those guys are cowering behind the bar. Waiting for a warrior to rescue them, even."

"I thought this was an adventurer hotspot," Nathan says.

"Tuesdays are slow," Hamish says.

"I draw my blade and charge! I slice at the kneecaps." I roll my d20. "Does a fifteen hit?"

"Sure does."

It's silly, but my heart picks up speed a little. I roll a d6 for my shortsword damage and add my Strength modifier of plus two. "Seven damage."

"Your blade wedges between the plates of the crabkind's natural armour and you slice at his meat," Hamish says.

Ian, who had the second-highest roll for initiative this battle, raises his hand, like he's in school. "Do we have to fight them? What if I talk to them?"

"You could," Hamish says.

"They don't exactly seem friendly," Rumour says. "All we know is they're barging into an adventurer bar looking for a fight."

When she speaks, a tingling wave of emotion washes over my body. Like when we're in the same class and she answers a question before I can. A moment of connection, our minds working on the same problem.

And just like at school, I stare at her from across the table until her eyes meet mine. Does she know I was staring? Does she know how badly I want to be her friend again? Does she think about me at all?

I hate having her here and I love having her here, and I can't focus over the rush of blood in my ears.

"I did already attack them," I speak up, feeling a little guilty. I didn't even think to handle this peacefully. "We haven't officially met, though. You can leave me to meet my crustacean fate."

Ian shakes his head. "No way, we're sticking together! I cast Unseen Servant, and uh . . . Unseen Servant can't attack, can it?"

"Afraid not," Hamish says. "But it can do plenty with a little *imagination.*" He moves his hands in front of his face in an arc, like we're supposed to imagine a rainbow between his palms.

Ian picks at his cloak. "Uh . . . okay, I got it! I tell the Unseen Servant to curl up behind the legs of a crab guy. Then someone can push him over! Is that allowed?"

"Classic schoolyard bullying," Hamish says. "We'll say that gives him disadvantage on all rolls. Anything else?"

"I use my bonus action to give Ashley Goldielocks Bardic Inspiration," Ian says, finishing his turn.

"Oakley Goldenrod," I correct him, unsure if I'm being teased by a ten-year-old. "But thank you."

Hamish clucks his tongue. "You're a fast learner, kid. Journey, you get another d6 to add to your rolls. Single use until Jace here uses Bardic Inspo again. You're up, Greta."

Greta smirks into her knitting. "Me? Smashwell is so into her book, she doesn't even notice the action."

Nathan mumbles a prayer. "Myrkul, god of death, make it quick."

"Aw, you love me," Greta says. "Anyway, my turn's over. Carry on."

"Everyone stand back," Nathan says, shaking a d20 in his hand. "I'm going to fire an arrow straight into the heart of the closest crabkind."

Nathan throws his d20. It bounces on the table, against a glass, and then flies through the air. It hits the floor and refuses to stop until it bumps against a table leg across the room. Nathan's cockiness vanishes.

"Your dice are cursed," Hamish says.

"Don't say that," Nathan basically whimpers.

Ian raises his hand again. "His dice hit the floor. Shouldn't he reroll?"

"What do you think, Nathan?" Hamish says. "You think maybe last campaign you shouldn't have fought so hard to keep your nat-floor-twenty? You think maybe you died on the wrong hill for a house rule?"

"I am nothing without my integrity," Nathan says. "Get it over with."

Hamish crouches over the rogue die. "My friend . . . that's a nat one."

Nathan throws his head back and howls, "NOOOOO —!"

Cradling the die like an injured bird, Hamish takes slow steps back to the table. "Ra'ven Tor'el nocks an arrow, aims at the crabkind — and slips on a puddle of ale. His own hand smacks himself in the face and he tumbles backward. The arrow sticks into the ceiling. The crabkind laugh at him. He is now supine."

Nathan slumps over with his face hidden in his folded arms. His howl quiets into a moan of devastation.

"When you're finished grieving," Hamish says, "please roll for fall damage. Tragically, the Clawbertons take their turn before the last member of our party."

Rumour shrugs. "No worries."

Hamish rolls for all five enemies. Jace the Bard takes two damage from a water attack that squirts from one crab's mouth. ("Ewww," he says, wincing.) Smashwell Stronk takes four damage from a chair thrown at her, and she puts away her book. Oakley dodges the first attack thrown their way. Nathan takes psychic damage from the crabkind ignoring Ra'ven supine on the floor because he doesn't seem like a threat.

The last crabkind saves the worst for Rumour. Hamish rolls and immediately looks sorry. "That's a twenty. Sebastian Clawberton crits."

"Jesus," Nathan murmurs.

"Oh no," Greta says.

"Big oof," Rumour says casually.

"A crit means he attacks twice." Hamish rolls two attack dice. "But that wasn't too bad. Five."

"My HP is only six," Rumour says. "I guess I'm almost dead."

My heart skips a beat. Rumour can't drop in the first round of the first battle. She might fail her death saves and spend the rest of the night waiting at another table.

I double-check my character sheet. I have the move Protection, giving enemies disadvantage with my shield. I can ready my action to protect her.

For Ian, of course. The more fun his sister has, the more fun he'll have.

"There's still time," Hamish says. "Last turn of the round. What'll it be, Demonica?"

06 The Most Holy Temple of . . . Red Lobster?

BLEEDING FROM HER WOUNDS, *Demonica Scribe climbs atop a wobbly table. She casts a spell both famous and infamous. "Magic missile!"*

Three glowing darts of magic flash from her fingertips. They cross the room in a blink and throw the crabkind who hit her back out the front door. Smoke rises from the embers in their chest.

"Bravo." Smashwell puts a hand on Demonica's shoulder. "Allow me to cure your wounds."

"Thanks," Demonica says.

Oakley scurries to Demonica's side. They raise their short sword and buckler. "Oakley Goldenrod. Pleasure to fight by your side."

"Don't do that," Demonica says.

"What?"

"Go away. I don't need your protection."

"Um, is this in-game, or . . . ?"

Demonica groans and rolls her eyes.

Ra'ven sets up another shot, aiming for the eye stalks of a Clawberton. He misses his planned shot, but at least hits the enemy this time, wedging an arrow between their chest plate and shoulder.

"They have too much armour!" Jace calls. "They have to have a weakness . . ."

Ian scrunches up his face like he's moving around memories, searching for one packed up in a box at the bottom of a pile. His fingers tap the table.

Rumour grins like she's seen him do this to the

point where it's a running joke in their house.

Then, he shouts, "Red Lobster!"

"They're crabs, buddy," Rumour says.

"Same thing! Monsters have weaknesses, right? Like Pokémon? Are crabs weak to butter?"

"There's no Red Lobster in Pan-Terra," Nathan says. "Or butter-type Pokémon. And this is clearly metagaming."

"Let the child metagame a little, as a treat," Greta says.

"It's about the integrity of the game," Nathan says.

Instead of participating, I'm thinking about when Rumour snapped at me. I was only trying to help because her *character* was injured! Am I not allowed to interact with her at all? Would she have a better time if I just left? Nausea churns in my gut, like I'm stuck in a spinning carnival teacup of anxiety.

I gotta pull it together. If I can't be chill with Rumour, I can at least keep backing up Ian. "We're in a seaside town. Jace probably had seafood with butter at some point."

Unsuccessfully hiding his laughter behind the partition, Hamish says, "Go ahead and roll a Wisdom check to see if Jace knows crabs are weak to butter. I'll say you can do it with advantage, which means you get to roll twice and pick the higher number."

Ian lets his d20 tumble from his palm once, then rolls a second time. "Seventeen!"

"I hate this," Nathan says.

"Here's what Jace knows . . ." Hamish says.

Jace hesitates as if listening to some higher power explain his own lore to him. "I spent a year playing music for the monks at the . . . the Holy Temple of the . . . Crimson . . . Crusty — Crustash —"

"Crustacean," Demonica says.

"Yeah, that thing," Jace says. "We need something that can get into their cracks. We need boiling butter!"

Jace strums on his lute, summoning a flash of magical light that forms into a floating Mage Hand. The hand flies to the kitchen and grabs a pot and a stick of butter.

"It needs to be hot!"

"I'll cast Fire Bolt on it," Demonica says, dashing into the kitchen.

Oakley and Ra'ven fight back the Clawbertons. Sword clashes against claw. Arrows bounce away harmlessly and fall to the floor.

"Let me know when you need Healing Word!" Smashwell calls, clutching her book to her barrel chest.

"I'd prefer you use your mace to bash their heads in," Ra'ven growls.

"Love you too!"

"We demand vengeance against the chef who destroyed our island," Sebastian Clawberton says again. "Lower your arms or face the wrath of the mighty seaAAARRRGH —"

Boiling butter rains on the crabkind. Sebastian Clawberton falls to his knees in agony. Another crabkind slips and cracks his head against the table. The remaining two impale themselves on their weapons.

Sebastian Clawberton knocks over a chair with a final twitch of his leg.

"Can't believe the butter thing worked," Ra'ven grumbles.

A slow clap sounds from behind the bar. The old man with the feather approaches the warriors. "Impressive fighting, my friends. If I may, I was wondering if you might reconsider my job offer."

Ra'ven rises to meet him. "What kind of job —"

He slips in the spreading butter puddle, hitting the ground hard beside the fallen enemies. "What did I do to deserve this fate?"

Smashwell grabs him by the front of his shirt and lifts him back to his feet, cloak dripping. "Lucky you don't have a concussion."

"I have misplaced an important book," the quest-giver continues. "A day's journey from here, I was investigating an abandoned temple. I'm a writer, you see, and I'm compiling a book of forgotten cuisine in our little corner of the continent."

"You're writing a cookbook?" Jace says excitedly.

"Just so! It's why I'm here to see the famed Chef Laios. Alas, I must have forgotten my book at the temple, or perhaps dropped it on the road."

"Why are you looking for recipes in abandoned temples?" Oakley asks.

"Every religion has its offering to their gods, and food is sacred," the man says. "Sadly for those of the abandoned temples, it seems their offerings were not enough to save their gods. I only wish to keep safe their knowledge."

"No offence," Smashwell says, "but why don't you just turn back and get it yourself?"

"I'm sure I need not tell you how dangerous the roads have become. Used to be a quick prayer would keep us safe. Between the bandits and the monsters, I hardly made it to The Silly Goose at all."

Thunder rumbles, shaking the walls.

"Say we do this job," Demonica says. "What's in it for us?"

"A good deal of gold, of course," says the stranger. "Five hundred gold pieces, should you accept the task. Five hundred more once you return with my property. Do we have a deal?"

"Quest time!" Jace says.

"We don't even know each other," Oakley says. "First we need to agree to being a team."

"All who wish to embark on this journey together," Smashwell says, "say 'aye.'"

A chorus of "aye" rings out, along with Ra'ven's single "I guess."

"What are we called?" Jace asks, bouncing on his heels with excitement. "The Fellowship of the Book? The Mighty Crabslayers? The Silliest Gooses?"

"Geese," Ra'ven corrects.

"We'll figure it out later." Oakley offers a hand to the man. "I think we have a deal, Mister . . . ?"

"Master Petrin, if you please." He passes a coin purse to Oakley, as well as a map. "The Temple of the Chimera is marked accordingly. Do hurry. This cookbook is my life's work."

With that, Master Petrin retires to his room upstairs.

"Creepy dude," Demonica says under her breath.

"Most dudes with money are," Smashwell says.

"We should probably have a long rest before we go," Oakley says. "Can we afford it?"

"Your coin is no good here," comes a voice from the kitchen. Chef Laios is trembling and covered in sweat,

but relief is clear on his face. "I was an adventurer once myself, before I took a pincer to my knee. Now I am old and retired. I would surely have met Lady Death today were it not for your help. Please, enjoy your stay free of charge. Oh, and one more thing."

He goes further into the kitchen. Pots clatter. Knives scrape. A single dish shatters. The chef returns holding a small chest of wood and leather. "I want you to have this. I cannot thank you enough for your actions today."

"Nope!" Ra'ven says.

"What's wrong?" Greta asks, as Nathan shoves back from the table.

"Last campaign, Hamish swore he'd get me with a mimic when it was his turn to DM," Nathan says.

"That was just a joke," Hamish says. "I can't make every treasure chest a mimic."

"It won't matter because I am careful. Cunning."

"Paranoid?"

"You're trying to get me."

"No metagaming," Greta chides.

"I'm *not* opening that chest," Nathan says.

"Will no one accept Chef Laios's generous gift?" Hamish asks.

"I'll take it," Rumour says.

"Demonica opens the chest to reveal what seems to be a normal satchel. Seeing your confusion, the chef explains," and here Hamish puts back on his Chef Laios voice, deeper pitched and nasally. "'It's a bag of holding! Not exactly rare, I know, but I hope it's useful.'"

Rumour flashes a dazzling smile. "I think I'm starting to like this game."

07 The Unavoidable Distraction of Side Quests

"THE PARTY LEAVES The Silly Goose at dawn," Hamish says. "They travel north by foot for a day and a night. The roads are dusty from heat and thirsty for rain, and emptier than they should be. It's as if the disappearance of the gods scared away friendly faces and bandits alike . . ."

My attention wanders, much like our characters. Hunched over my character sheet, I run my pencil over my sketch, shading Oakley's hair and poorly crosshatching shadow on their face.

I'd hoped by this point Rumour and I would reach a silent agreement to sweep our history under the rug. At least for tonight. But after she snapped at me, every word I speak feels like it might activate a trap card.

I'm sorry for every time I glance at her. For every skip of my heartbeat. For my secret delight in the sweet smell of her perfume. For every response as Oakley that she takes the wrong way.

I'm sorry for the last three and a half years.

But I can't tell her. Not here. Maybe not ever. Because she doesn't want to hear it. Because it's too many years too late.

"I bet the book is more valuable than he let on," Rumour says, and I'm dragged out of my moping. Her voice always had that effect on me. "Petrin seemed like a creep. I say we don't go back."

"We accepted a quest," Nathan says. "Where is your honour?"

"What do you care about honour? Aren't you supposed to be some sort of rogue?"

"I'm a *ranger*. I have a *code*."

"A code you'd abandon as soon as a goblin crosses our path," Greta says.

I think our characters are taking a break? We haven't done anything we'd need a short rest to recover from. I listen for context clues, feeling my face heat up a little. There's no way I could explain with "My bad, I zoned out because I can't stop thinking about how much I need Rumour's approval."

"Would anyone like some stale bread?" Ian asks. I guess we're eating? "The bacon should almost be done, too."

"Why are we doing this?" Nathan says.

"It's called *roleplaying*, sweetie," Greta says. "I would love a strip of bacon, Jace."

"Did somebody say bacon?" Clive shouts from the kitchen.

"We're good, Clive!" Hamish says. "Let's say the bacon is done. Roll for crispiness."

Ian tosses his d20. "Uh oh. Is seven bad?"

"The fire cooks your bacon unevenly. The strips

are somehow undercooked and too crispy at the same time. Jace wonders if maybe the perfect bacon doesn't exist anywhere but in his dreams."

"Aw, man."

"Suddenly, a squeaky voice reaches you from the road. 'Excuse me, fair travellers!' An orange cat in a pointy hat and dusty robes toddles downhill to your camp. A large bag sways on his back."

Greta drops her knitting, hands smacking her cheeks in joy. "A talking cat! What a cutie!"

In his cat voice, Hamish says, "'I am not a cutie. I am a wizard.'"

"Even cuter!"

"Another random NPC?" Nathan says. "Suspicious."

"'Random NPCs wander this main road all the time!'" Hamish squeaks. "'I am Magician Mittens!'"

Rumour and Ian both sit up straighter, eyebrows raised. My stomach drops.

Be careful when you're friends with a writer. Any argument you have can appear in their next book. Reading their stories, you'll look for parallels to their real lives. Or find the obvious self-inserts. Or pick up hints about what they think of *you*.

And I know exactly where Hamish got this idea.

"That's weird," Ian says, his tone hollow. "That's my cat's name."

Hamish clears the squeakiness from his voice. "Weird coincidence! Give him a head pat for me."

"He's dead now," Ian says.

". . . Oh."

Hamish stole Mittens from my and Rumour's *King of Coats* roleplay. We made up the part for Ian. Hamish thought he was being clever with this new attempt at meddling in my business. But Magician Mittens is a puppet made of half-remembered trivia tangled up in my real life, and Hamish is carelessly pulling whatever strings he can reach.

When the game is over, I'm lecturing him on the ethics of Original Character theft. Right after I'm finished ranting about the ethics of using necromancy on dead friendships.

Hamish's pale face has turned a violent shade of red,

making the blue in his hair really pop. He finally catches my glare and has the decency to look ashamed, at least. "I'm sorry. We can change the name if you want."

Ian either lets Rumour rub his back or is so upset that he forgets to stop her.

"No, it's . . . it's nice," Ian says. "I can remember him whenever I think about the first time I played *Dungeons & Dragons*. Two of my favourite things."

Spluttering, Hamish tries to pick up where he left off. "'I — I saw your brave band of adventurers from the road and was hoping I could point you to a growing problem in the area. Just the job for Good Samaritans such as yourself.'"

"There are Bible references in Pan-Terra?" Nathan says.

"'Did I say Good Samaritan?'" Hamish says as Mittens. "'I meant Great Salmon-itan, Patron Saint of Raw Fish. Anyway! There is a nearby colony of goblins just an hour east from here, squatting in an empty mine. The locals have lost many precious items in the goblin attacks. What do you say?'"

"This is a distraction," Nathan says.

"But Mittens needs our help," Ian says. "I vote for the side quest!"

"*D&D* needs a minimum age cap," Nathan says.

"Hey, now," Rumour snaps. Ian turns to her with a frown, shaking his head. She takes a breath before suggesting, "I think we should get experience points before we end up at the temple and have to fight a boss battle. Besides, Jace is our fearless leader —"

"*Jace*?" Nathan demands. "*Jace the Bard* is our leader?"

Ian gives a great big smile, showing off the spaces where his last two adult teeth struggle to sprout.

"Is there somebody else you had in mind?" Rumour says.

"Anybody else!" Nathan says.

"Isn't your whole deal that you want to fight goblins?" I ask. "Why aren't you pro-fighting goblins?"

"That's not the point!" Nathan says.

"It is why we were at The Silly Goose," Greta says.

"It's pretty metagamey of you not to go after your

main motivation." I hold up a hand. "I also vote for the side quest."

"You don't have to just because we are," Rumour says. "You're your own person."

It's like Rumour cast Mage Hand to slap me in the face. Why can't I do anything right tonight? I resist the strong urge to crawl under the table.

Damn Hamish for doing this to me. Damn him for even giving me this job.

"Why aren't you letting Journey be on my side?" Ian asks, turning to look at Rumour. "Aren't you on my side?"

"Of course I am. They just don't *have* to take your side if it's some weird game."

"It's not," I say, holding up both hands in surrender.

"Looks like my vote doesn't count for much," Greta says, cutting through the tension I seem to be causing, "but goblins are, in fact, your whole deal, babe. I won't be killing anyone, but let's see if we can't put the fear of the Silliest Geese into them."

"I did *not* agree to that name," Nathan says, crossing his arms.

"It was literally your idea," Greta says.

"I just said the plural of *goose* is not *gooses* —"

"'Wonderful!'" says Hamish as Magician Mittens. "'I'll wait here until you have finished.'"

08 White Knighting

"TIME FOR EVERYONE'S FAVOURITE part of *D&D*," Hamish says, leaning toward Nathan, "more background info!"

"It's not my first favourite," Ian says, "but it might be third or fourth!"

"At least someone appreciates me. Ahem. As everyone in Pan-Terra knows . . ."

. . . the dwarven mines were commissioned by the Queen of Reignem. The human kingdom had plenty of fertile ground for farming but needed precious minerals. Meanwhile, the dwarves had plenty of ore and jewels, but their diet was mostly the root vegetables and the non-poisonous monsters found in the mines. A trade deal was agreed upon.

They eventually had to abandon the project when the mines were used as passageways for demons in the Dark Emperor's army. Unfortunate for the truce between human and dwarf, but quite fortunate for the goblins who moved in after.

Though goblins keep to the shadows of the realm, Ra'ven finds goblin tracks in the flattened grass (though he does fall out of a tree attempting to get the high ground). The tracks lead to the mouth of a cave, dwarven-made with wooden support beams arcing along the stone. Rusty, abandoned pickaxes lay where they fell, left behind.

The cave drops steeply downward, into the mountain and the darkness. Not everyone has darkvision, so Oakley pulls a torch from their explorer's pack. A persistent dripping echoes through the cave.

"Stay behind me," Ra'ven says. "I'll check for traps —"

There's a heavy thunk.

"Tell me you didn't," Demonica says.

An arrow whips from the darkness and lodges into the wall above Oakley's head.

"If I was any taller, you'd have killed me!" Oakley cries.

Ra'ven removes his foot from the sunken pressure plate. "Remind me to buy you platform boots."

"Don't worry, little one," says Smashwell as she scoops Oakley up like a baby. "I will protect you with my beefy bod."

With strong green arms wrapped around them, Oakley mumbles, "Uh, thanks?"

"I can walk in front," Jace says.

"Absolutely not. At least now we know what we're looking for —" Ra'ven is again interrupted as he trips forward and lands flat on his face. There's a snap of wire, and from deep in the mountain, an explosion of clanging bells.

"Yikes," says a raspy voice in the shadows.

Two figures approach, close enough for Oakley's torchlight to reveal green skin and yellow eyes.

"You made this very easy for us," says the goblin, hand on her weapon. "The whole colony will be here soon."

Hamish leans forward, resting his bearded chin on his knuckles. "Nathan, I really don't want to kill you, but your rolls are not making it easy."

"This is my villain origin story," Nathan says, facing the ceiling with his head on the back of the chair.

Greta kisses his cheek. "Aw, hun, I think you'll have to go a bit further back . . ."

"What happens now?" Ian asks.

"That's up to you," Hamish says. "You've been caught sneaking into the goblin colony. What do you Silly Geese want to do?"

"Please stop," Nathan says.

"Don't worry, guys," Ian says. "I'll convince them to let us go."

"Um, why would they do that, bud?" Rumour asks. "We're here to kill them."

"They don't know that," Ian says.

"Won't you feel bad tricking them into letting us go, only to stab them in the face?" she asks.

Ian deflates. "Well, now I do."

"You can still try," I offer. "You don't need to lie about our kindness or whatever, but maybe your bard magic can stun them or freak them out."

Ian nods along. "Yeah, okay. Jace sings a death metal song that surprises the goblins so much, they drop their weapons."

"You should be singing, then," Nathan says.

We all turn to him. As usual, his face is motionless, unreadable. I never really know when he's making a joke. Or if he even makes jokes.

Wide-eyed, Ian's grin wilts. He looks around for help. "D-Do I need to?"

"You chose to be a bard, but you haven't sung a note," Nathan says. "Why are you a bard if you aren't going to make any effort?"

"Hold up, dude," Rumour says, "how about you back o —"

There's a thump under the table. The tabletop shakes, rattling forks over plates and splashing tea from mugs. Rumour's cheek twitches. She finishes her sentence with a whispered, "*Owww* . . ."

Hanging out with the two of them for the last hour and a half, it's obvious that Ian wants the safety of Rumour's presence. He also wants independence from her.

But I'm not his sister. I'm nothing but a fellow tabletop gamer who made a vow to back him up when the trolls arrived.

I can't be a wallflower.

"Ian doesn't need to sing," I say. "Unless he wants to."

"Then what's the point?" Nathan says.

"To have fun," I say firmly. "You know what's not fun? For any of us? Nerdy gatekeepers telling younger fans they're doing things wrong."

"It's just a game, Nate," Greta says, knitting needles clacking together. "Your *Dungeons* integrity is starting to look more like bullying a child."

"Tween," Ian corrects her. "And I'll be eleven in five months!"

"Apologies, little dude," she says. "Bullying a tween."

"The official ruling from me," Hamish says, "your humble gaming god, is that this is a make-believe game and the real-life people should feel comfortable. Do what you like as long as you're having fun and causing no harm."

Ian scoots back from the edge of his seat, relaxing.

"Fine," Nathan says. "If you won't commit, I will."

"You're going to do a backflip trick shot with a bow and arrow, right here, right now?" Rumour says.

Nathan pinches his metal d20, narrowing his eyes like it owes him money. "I'm going to slaughter these goblins."

Ra'ven dodge-rolls backward, nocks an arrow, and releases it. The arrow whistles through the air, bounces off the wall, and lodges into the thigh of the goblin on the left. She screams and drops to the ground. The other goblin draws their blade.

"Intruders!" the goblin cries, their voice echoing down the tunnels, before they lunge at Demonica. The rusty edge of their weapon slashes open her cheek as she stumbles backward, caught off-guard. The goblin swings a second time.

Oakley leaps into the arc of the goblin's sword. They knock it out of the way and lunge for the goblin's neck —

"Stop it!" Rumour stands so fast her chair falls over, loudly clattering to the floor. "Stop trying to protect me!"

"What?" I say, even as my entire head buzzes with anxiety. "I'm just trying to — I mean, Oakley just wants to be a good teammate, and . . . and, you know, make friends."

"Are you serious right now?" Rumour says, narrowing her eyes.

I shrink under her glare. "It's part of their motivation?"

"Whatever."

Rumour spins around and storms outside, into the snowfall. The room seems to stretch, the door growing further away. Hands flat on the tabletop, my heartbeat pulses through my fingertips as if infusing the wood with waves of heartache.

I can practically feel my hit points plummeting. The one-heart-remaining video game alarm beeps in my mind. Seconds away from one final "Mamma mia" before Bowser burns the Mushroom Kingdom to the ground.

"Really? The one time my dice cooperate," Nathan grumbles.

"There, there, babe," Greta says, patting the top of his head.

Hamish blows out a breath through puffed cheeks. Looks like he's run out of clever ways to force me and Rumour together.

Ian wraps a loose string from his cloak around his index finger and tugs. It comes loose. He says nothing.

Rumour's abrupt exit leaves us like a broken family

at Thanksgiving, mid-argument about politics. Except somehow I'm the weird uncle making the situation uncomfortable. Or whatever the gender-neutral term for uncle is, anyway.

I . . . really messed up. I keep throwing myself at Rumour like we can just be friends. Maybe I need a gentler approach to co-existing with her.

Or a more honest one.

I stand up. "I'm gonna check on her."

"How about we all take a five-minute snack break?" Hamish suggests. "I think Clive might die from loneliness if we don't."

09 Wow, You Can Fit so Much Baggage in This Bag of Holding!

IT'S TOO COLD TO BE OUTSIDE without a full snowsuit. Clearly, Rumour feels the same way. She sits on the curb in a pile of snow several centimetres higher than it was an hour ago, holding herself and shivering despite her winter coat.

"Hey," I say.

She doesn't respond.

I step to her side and hesitate only a moment before I sit in the snow too. The cold instantly freezes my butt. An unpleasant wetness follows.

An inch of space separates us, but so does a gulf of time. Years of wondering and waiting, of guilt and shame. We haven't been this close since the day she confided in me.

The day I screwed it all up.

"I didn't mean to . . ." I stop the excuses from pouring out of my mouth. Instead, I release them in a cloud of condensation. "It doesn't matter what I meant. I'm sorry."

"No, I'm the one being weird," Rumour says. "You didn't actually do anything . . ."

A lump hardens in my throat. It would be so easy to take the out she's offering. To avoid making things right and go back to a life without Rumour in it. But that's not what I want.

"Not just tonight," I tell her. "I'm sorry about everything. I'm sorry I hurt you."

Rumour stares into the parking lot. A flurry of snowflakes take the spotlight under the glow of a streetlamp.

Exposed, my arms and cheeks burn from the cold. My fingers lose feeling, and I stuff them under my armpits. At least I was already wearing a winter hat for the aesthetic.

"You protecting me in this game feels *wrong*," she says. "It's just a game and I know you're not doing it to hurt me, but it makes me angry. Like, you didn't protect me. For all of high school."

It's like a punch in the face I knew was coming — that I offered up, while saying, "You get one free hit."

"You're right," I say. "I should have put my skill points into being a better friend."

She snorts, lowering her brief smile into her puffy pink sleeves. "You're still such a dork."

"A really, really sorry dork."

"It would have hurt less if you'd just told me you were done. Made it official. But you didn't do that. You avoided me and made excuses and ghosted me until I stopped trying."

Her voice catches in her throat, snagging on a shard of the pain I caused. Now, finally, she faces me. Her teary eyes glow pink in the neon light of the Limited Series sign. "I have to know why. Why did you drop me like that? When I needed you most . . ."

I take a deep breath, trembling from anxiety and cold. "I was afraid. I came out in grade ten. A whole year after ghosting you. A year of overthinking, experimenting, trying out pronouns online. You were so sure of yourself so much earlier than me."

"That only makes me more confused. It's not like you came out, tracked me down, and apologized. You don't even acknowledge me at school. Seeing you here tonight . . . This has been really painful."

The lump returns to my throat. A threat of tears to come. I'm only making more excuses. Shielding myself from having to feel the full weight of my guilt.

"It's painful for me too," I say, quieter than the snowflakes pelting the street.

"A real apology would include a real explanation."

Braving the cold, I take off my hat so my frozen fingers can curl around the *King of Coats* emblem. Draw strength from it.

"All I knew about queer culture was that bullies called me gay to hurt me," I say. "And it worked. Or they called me a girl to insult me and it pissed me off. Even when my parents tried supporting me by being 'open-minded' or whatever, I just hated people assuming things about me. So I didn't let myself think about it.

"When you told me you felt like you'd been forced into being a boy against your will, that it was making you really unhappy — I felt the same way. But you actually wanted to do something about it, and I didn't think I was allowed to. I had a lot of confusing feelings. Jealousy was definitely one of them. I let those feelings turn me into the worst best friend ever."

"You think I didn't have all the same problems you had and then some? We had all the same bullies, were called all the same names — except for where we were different, Journey. Try going through all the same shit and being Black."

"I know. I was never as strong as you."

"Taking more abuse doesn't make me stronger."

"Living truthfully despite it does."

"Yeah, well, that's the only part I can control," she says. "Even knowing a lot of girls like me get hurt for it, in a lot worse ways than I've been hurt, it's all I can do. I wish I didn't have to be strong. I just want to live my life."

Gripping my hat, I hold myself back from the strongest desire I've ever had to give someone a hug.

"For what it's worth," I say, "it didn't take me long to realize pushing you away was the worst choice ever. In, like, all of human history. But I don't think I could've been a safe person for you until I'd figured out how to be a safe person for myself. As soon as I came to terms with all my gender stuff, the first person I wanted to tell was you. I just . . . couldn't. I'd screwed up too big."

"You did screw up pretty big." After a moment, Rumour adds, "But not *too* big."

She looks at me again in a way that lights a fire beneath my skin, banishing the chill.

"Why 'Journey?'" she asks.

"I guess because I'm on one. It felt kinda like

I was Bilbo Baggins. 'I'm going on an adventure!' You know?" I laugh through my nose, waiting for her to make fun of me. She doesn't, so I ask, "Why 'Rumour'?"

"I guess . . . to have some power over them. Plus, *Umbrella Academy* is my jam. Looks like we're still a couple of pretentious nerds, even apart."

We deserve each other, I want to say.

"I love *Umbrella Academy*," I say instead, like a coward. "Klaus gives me major gender envy."

Rumour raises an eyebrow. She looks at me like she's picturing me in eyeliner and a mesh top. I put my toque back on like it'll stop her from reading my mind.

"How'd your parents take the news?" she says.

"The gayest thing my mom is into is *Queer Eye*. Which, to be clear, isn't nothing. I owe Jonathan Van Ness a life debt. My dad had a bit more trouble, but he's like an OG *D&D* guy who's always talking about the Satanic Panic. So I told him I'm multi-classing gender. I have levels in both Girl and Boy." I'm rambling, which isn't helped by the lost mobility in my freezing lips. "How about yours?"

"They didn't freak out or anything, but they had a lot to learn. They made some rookie mistakes." Rumour stretches out her legs, kicking aside accumulated snow with her pink Converse. "Stuff like crying about losing their son. Discomfort with hormones and surgery. Confusion about how this even happened, since they never gendered my toys or clothes. The worst was when they blamed themselves for every bit of harassment I'd get, from kids at school or randos in public bathrooms.

"But when I gave them queer books, they read them. When I sent them links to trans YouTubers, they watched hours-long video essays. We saw a specialist in Toronto who put me on puberty blockers and then on estrogen. Even though they didn't always understand me, my parents tried really hard to help me anyway. That's the most important thing. They respected me and trusted that I knew myself better than anyone. I'm really lucky. These days, my parents talk about pre-transition like they should have known. Really, the way I always wanted to be Princess Cassandra should have been a red flag. Or a blue, pink, and white flag."

"You really had me convinced it was because she had the best magic." The warmth in my chest grows my smile like rich soil for a blooming flower. A secret springtime lurking inside me despite winter's best efforts. "I'm happy you figured yourself out. I wish I could have been there to help."

"I wish you could have been, too."

"Is it too late to start?"

My heart is pounding so hard, but I don't know if it's because of Rumour's smile or because the poor organ is trying not to let me die in a snowbank. I shouldn't feel so flustered. We've only just repaired a friendship, and I really don't want this stupid crush to ruin it before it's rebuilt. I hurt her so much. I barely know her anymore. What I have a crush on is the idea of her, made of memories and images.

Holding hands, facing down a thunderstorm.

It's not real, not anymore. I shove my crush deep down inside, hoping it'll melt in my stomach acid like a magic ring in lava. Restoring hope to Middle-Earth. Or Pan-Terra, rather.

"You can start by helping me up," Rumour says. "I can't feel my butt."

"I can't feel any part of my body."

I stand, my legs weirdly hollow in their numbness, and I hold out my hand.

She takes it.

10 Who Inspires the Bards?

WE HEAD INSIDE, soaking wet and shivering. The warm blast of café air is a relief, until the feeling returns to my fingers. They tingle painfully.

"Clive, your time has come!" I say. "We need two hot chocolates, stat!"

"Sorry," Clive says, leaning on the countertop, "we don't sell 'hot chocolates.' Try the Tim's down the street."

"Did I say hot chocolate? I meant two Better ChocoLate Than Nevers."

Satisfied, Clive says, "Coming right up."

When I turn to Rumour, she's smiling. Not at me, exactly, but beside me. With me.

Clive passes me a small Pokéball for the same reason he won't sell me a normal hot chocolate. The man loves his ceremony. Rumour and I drag our soggy feet to the gaming room. The round table is missing one extra player.

Ian isn't there.

Gesturing to his seat, Rumour says, "Washroom?"

"Didn't say," Hamish says. "Please tell me we didn't lose a kid."

Rumour jabs a finger at Nathan. I've never seen acrylic nails look deadlier. "If you were an asshole to him while I was gone, you better watch your back."

Nathan sinks in his chair. "I don't think I did anything?" Without breaking eye contact with Rumour, he reaches for Greta. "Did I?"

"You deserve whatever torture she decides on," Greta says, keeping her hands, eyes, and sympathy on the yarn in her lap.

I turn around, back to the retail room. Ian stands in front of the wall of action figures, long cloak stretched taut along his back. My favourite section too. I spent way too much of my last paycheque on hundred-dollar action figures. (In my defence, they come with a bunch of extra pieces and also, so many joints!)

We must have walked right past him.

"Looks like he's browsing," I say.

Rumour sighs, retracting her claws. "I'd better go talk to him."

"I'll come." Thinking about the tension my offers of help caused today, I add, "If you want."

"Yeah. Okay."

When we reach Ian, he's staring into the empty black eyeholes of a poseable Jack Skellington. His cloak bunches in front of him and a thread is caught between his teeth. I don't think the set of his jaw and the pink tint of his eyes are from a staring contest.

Rumour reaches for his shoulder. "We good?"

Ian shakes his head. "You suck at promises," he says, his voice thick and strained from the clear effort of holding back tears.

"Did you think we were leaving early? I'm sorry I worried you. Journey and I just needed to chat. Like, *badly*."

Her words give me hope. Maybe I haven't fixed us for good, but I think she wanted our friendship repaired as much as I did. My shame was the only thing standing in our way, and I just rolled a natural 20 to decimate it.

But then Ian says, "I don't mean you."

I tear my gaze and my gooey feelings away from Rumour. He's talking about me.

Kneeling beside him, I say, "I'm sorry I left, too. But we're back to beat some goblins. We'll stick together this time."

"I don't care about some stupid game!" he yells, rounding on me. "I care that you disappeared!"

I flinch. "I don't know what —"

"I bet you think I don't remember you, but I do. I remember being so excited when you'd come over and bring your 3DS, and we'd all play that weird game that makes you shoot aliens with your faces on them."

"That was a very weird game," I say weakly.

"I remember when Rumour didn't want to bring me to the park, but you said you *needed* me."

"It was getting really hard to find alone time," Rumour says, just as weakly.

"I remember when you *promised*," Ian says.

His anger wipes the dust from half-forgotten memories. I remember too. And all I can think in response is, *Shit*.

Ian had come home from school devastated. He wouldn't tell his parents what was wrong. He wouldn't even talk to Rumour. But when I knocked on the door, he let me in. I sat on his bed while he told me every feeling banging on the door of his heart, begging to be let out.

Six years old and sobbing because his friend dumped him. Sweet, generous, funny Ian abandoned by some booger-eater who didn't deserve him. Some booger-eater who made Ian's stomach flutter with first-crush nervousness.

That day, I shared with Ian some difficult feelings of my own. Feelings I've never told Rumour. Feelings

I still clutch tightly, nestled between my ribs. And he made me promise I'd never leave.

A promise too easy to break.

When I lost Rumour, I also lost Ian. I loved him like family. I've been so focused on his sister, I didn't realize how badly I'd hurt this poor kid.

"I'm sorry, Ian," I say. "I really am."

Tears pour down his cheeks. "Why did you leave? Did we do something wrong?"

"It's totally my fault. You did nothing wrong, and neither did Rumour. I was just a jerk who had some things to figure out." Slowly, I reach out a hand to rest on his shoulder. He lets me. "I'd love to start hanging out again, if you still want me to."

He sniffles, long and wet. Palms wipe away tears, covering their tracks. "You promise?"

I squeeze his shoulder. "I promise."

"And you won't break it again?"

"Anything you want, any time. I'm there. You'll get so sick of how much I'll be there for you."

He practically leaps into my arms, almost knocking

me over. I catch the pink of Rumour's outfit in the corner of my eye. I wonder what she's thinking. How she feels about me. If I'm managing to be a better friend to them both.

I'll keep trying until I get it right. I'm not running away again.

"You know what I want?" Ian asks, releasing my neck.

"Tell me," I say.

Ian strikes a dramatic pose. One hand on his hip and the other pointing past me. "I want to finish this quest."

11 The Hoard of the Goblin Horde

"AS FORETOLD, OUR HEROES RETURN," Hamish says as we take our seats.

We must be a strange sight, all puffy-eyed and emotional. Then again, tears aren't that unusual during a tabletop gaming night. Ask any relationship therapist, they'll tell you *Monopoly* is the leading cause of divorce. *Catan* kills lifelong friendships. *Ticket to Ride* leads to purchasing one-way tickets. I could go on.

Clive places hot chocolate in front of me and Rumour. Ian swipes a finger through Rumour's whipped cream and plops it on his tongue.

"Nathan," Greta says in a warning tone, "is there something you would like to say?"

Nathan knits his eyebrows, glaring at his papers. Greta leans in super close to him, her face scrunching up.

"I don't know to what you refer," Nathan says, stuffier than usual.

I give Rumour a look, unsure how to explain what's happening. It's weird behaviour, even for them.

Hamish clears his throat, and begins again in his narrator voice. "Previously on The Silliest Geese, you had been captured by goblin guards. Alarms are going off. Before you can make any other moves, you're surrounded by thirty more goblins."

"Oakley Goldenrod is a monster hunter," I say. "I can take them."

"I assure you, you cannot," Hamish says.

"Since battles are so confusing, can Demonica

cast Disguise Self to look like one of the goblins?" Rumour asks.

"Uh, yeah, give me a Deception check," Hamish says.

"Sixteen."

"With practiced grace, the ever-more mysterious Demonica Scribe takes a step backward into the surrounding crowd of goblins. She disappears among them. A goblin counts your party, sure there had been more of you."

"Jace does that too!" Ian says.

"Because Demonica tried this trick first, roll with disadvantage," Hamish says. "Disadvantage is the opposite of advantage, so you pick the lowest of two rolls."

Ian rolls his d20 twice. He grimaces at the lower number. "Four."

"'Nice try, buddy,'" Hamish says in his nasally goblin voice.

"'This guy, am I right?'" Rumour says with a similar voice. "'He must think us fools, eh, fellow goblins?'"

Everyone at the table laughs, even Nathan. I smile at Rumour. She smiles back and shrugs.

"The goblins force you through their tunnels," Hamish says, "into a hidden city inside the mountain. Stalactites hang from the ceiling. Stalagmites stab upward from the floor. The goblin guards bring you across rope-bridges, to the throne of the Goblin King.

"His crown is made of a headband and a handful of mismatched forks. Draped over his shoulders is a robe that looks suspiciously like a housecoat, patterned with roses. Goblin commoners gather around, every one of them wearing unusual clothing and accessories, as if their wardrobe came from a garbage bag headed to Goodwill.

"'State your business,' says the Goblin King himself. 'What brings armed adventurers to my domain?'"

"Your Majesty," says Smashwell, dropping to one knee, "I confess, we were sent here to kill you. All of you."

A gasp washes over the crowd of goblin spectators. Someone boos. A slime cube is thrown at the party like a rotten tomato, splashing against the back of Ra'ven's head.

"What are you doing?!" Ra'ven demands.

"Answering their question?" the half-orc offers.

Ra'ven's face burns as hot as a glowing chunk of coal. "So lie!"

"Lying is a sin in the eyes of my gods, babe. Even though said gods are missing. I have a code, too."

"We are dead. It's over. Pack it up, people."

"Not to side with Ra'ven," Oakley says, "but I'd have liked the chance to lie."

"I could try saying it was just a joke?" Jace says.

"No one has enough Charisma to manage that," Ra'ven says. "Especially after everything we've said by now and are still saying."

The Goblin King narrows his yellow eyes. Slender green fingers tease apart the grey beard bundled in his lap. "And who sent you?"

Ra'ven snarls, "We'll never tell —"

"A wizard cat," Smashwell says, bringing one of her many notebooks to her face. She squints behind her glasses. "I have his name written down here . . . Mage Mutton?"

"Your handwriting is impressively bad," says a definitely random goblin from the crowd who was definitely there the whole time. A number of other goblins mutter in agreement.

"His name is Magician Mittens," Jace says.

"Thank you," Smashwell says. "Magician Mittens told us you were attacking nearby villages."

"I am not surprised," says the Goblin King, "but I am disappointed. We know the magician well. He is a wizard under an adorable yet unbreakable curse, exiled from his people. He lived in our community for many moons, using his magic to help us. He even brought us these fabulous items of clothing, claiming they were donations. But when Buckle found that blasted cookbook yesterday in the Temple of the Chimera, I saw the hunger in Mittens's eyes. This morning, both Mittens and the book had gone."

"It has to be the cookbook we're looking for!" Jace says, helpfully.

"Awfully convenient," Ra'ven grumbles.

"I don't think there's anything convenient about being sent on a wild goose chase," Smashwell says, pushing her glasses up her nose. "Ironic, though."

"So Mittens has the creepy old weirdo's book," Oakley says, counting plot twists on small fingers. "Which is either a magical item, or full of really great recipes. Where do the goblins fit in? Why does Mittens want you dead?"

"Alas," says the Goblin King, "I fear he only needs an easy scapegoat. Few adventurers would refuse an invitation to slay goblins —"

"Forget talking," Ra'ven says, "for it only breeds more lies. I'm doing this. FOR MY MOTHER, YOU BASTARDS!"

Ra'ven draws his knife and sprints toward the Goblin King. While the goblin guards all raise their weapons to stop the would-be assassin, one goblin simply sticks out their foot. Ra'ven trips on the goblin's bunny slipper and crashes to the ground.

"Um, I just want to make it clear that wasn't me," says a different, totally random goblin who definitely blends in.

"Your mother?" the Goblin King asks, unbothered.

"Apologies for my boyfriend's behaviour, Your Majesty," Smashwell says. "Goblins killed his parents. After that tragic day, he vowed to slay all of your kind. He's not known for changing his mind."

"Treachery," Ra'ven grumbles. "How dare you share my backstory with the enemy?"

The Goblin King tugs on his beard. "Believe me, I know the sting of tragedy. My husband was slain by a party of elves some years ago. You will notice I am not hunting all of elfkind to wear their ears around my neck, however." He sighs heavily, his body sinking into his throne. "I have been moved by the orc's sad tale of their clumsy boyfriend. Guards, free them."

"Look at what happens when you clearly communicate," Smashwell says, snapping her notebook shut with satisfaction.

"You're letting us go?" Oakley asks. "Just like that?"

"We require nothing in return," confirms the Goblin King.

"Pity, is it?" Ra'ven snarls, holding a knife in each hand and one in his teeth. "Fight me, you cowards!"

"We shall do no such thing. Instead, we offer only our deepest apologies. Truly, we are sorry about your family. We hope in time, you will see goblins are not all the same."

Ra'ven slumps, dropping his knives. "Why are you doing this to me?"

"It's going to be okay, babe," Smashwell says, rubbing his back. "Unlearn that goblin prejudice."

"I guess now we see if Mittens will give us the book," Oakley says.

"Wait!" Jace calls. "I adopt a goblin!"

"You what?" Hamish asks, laughing.

"Are there any goblin orphans?" Ian asks.

"Uh. Sure. Lots. A whole goblin orphanage."

"Let me adopt one please, goblins! I roll for, um . . . Persuasion check!"

"If you adopt a goblin, I will kill it," Nathan says.

"No, you will not," Greta says so firmly, I'm not surprised when Nathan mutters that he was only joking.

"Eleven!" Ian says. "Is that enough?"

"The head of the goblin orphanage approaches you from the crowd," Hamish says. "'Why should we allow you to take one of our own from the safety of our village?' she asks."

Ian bows his head and closes his eyes. "Because, Your Honour, I have always wanted a child to love as my own. The road is long and I've walked it alone for a long, lonely time. With my new family, the Silliest Geese, I think we'll give my goblin son a life of learning and excitement. And we can show the world that goblins are not scary or gross. You're people just like us!"

Hamish shrugs. "'Okay. You can have Kai. He keeps stealing from my bedroom, anyway.' A small, green-skinned goblin boy shuffles to the woman's side, his red hair a tangle of curls. A thumb sticks in his mouth. His other hand holds an old blankie."

"I love him," Ian says.

"How about you adopt two goblins," Rumour says. "I don't want to get left behind."

Hamish narrates, "As Demonica rejoins the team, a goblin wonders aloud if anyone recognizes her. Another whispers about how she's definitely going to die. The armed guards lead the party back outside the mountain."

"Is this going to be like when you swore you'd take care of Mittens but I ended up doing all the work?" Rumour asks.

"Probably more like when his Tamagotchi became your Tamagotchi because you were always babysitting it," I say.

"I guess I have a goblin now. Single mother of two," she says.

"I can be the cool, gender-neutral uncle."

"Gruncle Oakley."

"Hey, I was wondering earlier about the gender-neutral term for uncle," I say. "Gruncle feels good, feels right."

"I'm getting a bad feeling about this," Ian says. "Maybe you two should've stayed enemies."

"You're just reading our power levels," I say.

Rumour matches my goofy grin with one of her own. Except hers has the ability to liquefy my heart in my chest.

"Crush those scanners," she says. "It's over nine thousand."

12 The Most Dangerous Weapon

"HE'S GONE," *Ra'ven says as he examines the campsite.*

"Pretty sure we could tell without your rangerly insight," Demonica says, "but thank you anyway."

Indeed, the campsite is clearly deserted. The coals of the fire pit have long since cooled. The tents and supplies left with Magician Mittens have all been clawed to pieces.

"Since you find it so obvious," Ra'ven says shortly, "please tell me which direction he headed in."

Demonica surrenders. "You got me. Do your thing."

Ra'ven pinches earth and grass, and places it on his tongue. He chews, takes a big sniff, and brushes aside the leaves of a bush. Some of the branches are snapped. Ra'ven spits out the clump of chewed forest.

"This way," he says, leading the party further into the woods.

"It's about time your dice work," Greta says. Her once blobby yarn has become most of a scarf, draped over her shoulder.

"They know I'll throw them out if they act up again," Nathan says.

"Very normal of you, babe."

"Ra'ven's preferred terrain being the forest," Hamish says, "your party quickly tracks Mittens's paw prints over fallen trees and across ravines. At last the prints stop at a high rock wall with no sign that the wizard went around or climbed. The trail's gone cold."

"That's impossible," Ra'ven says, running his fingers along the stone.

"He is a wizard," Demonica says. "What's to stop him from just disappearing? Teleporting?"

"You tell me, wizard."

"Check for traces of magic," Oakley whispers from her side.

"Is that a thing I can do?" Demonica whispers back.

Sitting on a rock and tuning his lute, Jace gives her a thumbs up. On his right, Kai copies him with the thumb he isn't sucking.

"I'll cast Guidance," Smashwell says. "It'll give you a boost."

Demonica nods. "All right. I cast Detect Magic."

She holds her hands out to feel for traces of magic on the air. The space around her warps like a road on a hot summer day. The trees still their windy dance. The animals of the forest quiet their wild cries.

The rock wall trembles, casting off dust and pebbles

like shrugging off a coat. Rune etchings glow in the stone. When the glow fades, so does the entire cliff.

Casting aside the magic, Demonica reveals an old temple in the middle of a clearing. To either side of a wooden door, a wrap-around corridor has collapsed in on itself. Wild fiends have been carved into crumbled pillars: one-eyed beholders, panther-like displacer beasts, and winding dragons.

"The Temple of the Chimera," Demonica breathes. "It's been a while."

"Do you know it?" Oakley asks, joining her in front of the wooden door.

"I was raised in a temple just like this one."

"What! I can't believe you didn't tell me!" Jace cries. After a moment, he adds, "Even though we just met!"

"I've kept my past a secret for a long time. People can be cruel when they're scared. And plenty of rich and powerful people want you to be scared of me." Demonica runs a red hand through her hair, finding the sharp point of a horn. "The Cult of the Chimera was a tiefling church. We worshipped the ultimate symbol of changing

your nature. Of taking control of your fate. Becoming more than you ever thought you could."

I watch Rumour's face as she tells her story. She speaks so confidently, but I know from the impressed look on Hamish's face, she's making it up as she goes. She was always great at this part. A natural storyteller.

It's amazing getting to see her roleplay again, acting with such vulnerability. Using real pain she must have felt. It makes my heart ache. My cheeks flush with heat, and shame, and want.

I could love her. Fall so deep in love with her I never want to swim back to the surface, if she lets me.

If I let myself.

Rumour looks at me. I look at my hands, fingers clenched tight around a fistful of dice. I listen to her voice.

She draws me in like a siren.

"Our god was the first god to die because our church was Pan-Terra's biggest target. All it takes is one story about the Dark Emperor and his demons driving the dwarves from their mines. A single mention of their red skin and horns. No one cared that we had no wings. One story becomes many, traded at taverns, shared over dining halls, spreading like a sickness."

Demonica's fingers trace the outline of a carving. The teeth of a lion. "The night of the attack, we didn't stand a chance. Neither did the Chimera themself. As far as I know, that was when the war of the gods began. When the gods finally understood their most dangerous weapon. They all scrambled to use their followers to become the One and Only God . . . and because of their hunger for power, now there are none."

"Whoa," Jace whispers.

"You're incredible," Oakley says. "Uh, to have survived such hardship."

"I guess it's time for a part-demon to face her demons." Demonica grabs the doorknob and twists. It doesn't turn. The door rattles in place.

"Okay, that's extremely unfair," Oakley says. "The power of your speech alone should have unlocked the door."

"Better luck next time," Demonica says with a shrug and a shy smile.

"Stand back, everyone," Ra'ven says. "This is a job for Smashwell Stronk."

The half-orc looks up from the book she's reading. "I don't think I have any books on lock-picking."

"Kick down the door!" he growls. "Use your orc strength!"

"If you were paying attention, you would know my orc strength is underdeveloped!"

"Ugh, whatever. I'll do it myself."

Ra'ven steps forward and kicks the door. Nothing happens. He kneels before the doorknob and tries to pick the lock with his knives. Nothing continues to happen. After several minutes, he stands up and kicks a tree. Curiously, this also does not help.

"How hard could it be to pick a simple lock?" Demonica asks.

"Is it some kind of magic lock?" Jace asks.

"Must be," Ra'ven grumbles. "If only we had a rogue in the party."

"You know, my great-great-grand gruncle Baldo was a professional burglar," Oakley says.

"Yeah, yeah, everyone's got a rich backstory now," Ra'ven says.

While the Silliest Geese argue, Kai removes a cloth wrap of thieves' tools from hidden pockets inside his cloak. Sticking his tongue between his lips, he inserts a pair of squiggly-toothed picks into the rusty brass lock. He listens. Adjusts. Listens some more.

With a click, the door opens onto a dark passageway.

"My beautiful baby boy!" Jace says, scooping Kai up in a hug.

"Thank goodness we met those goblins and we all learned to respect them as people," Smashwell says. Her massive hand dwarfs Kai's head and she ruffles his curly hair.

Ra'ven grumbles, "I would've unlocked it eventually . . . "

Oakley draws their sword and equips their shield. "This feels like a boss fight. Are we ready?"

The rest of the party ready their weapons, prepare their spells, and join the halfling. They follow a warm, flickering light at the end of the hall and step into the temple.

Cobwebs hang from corners and dust coats every surface. Marble columns stretch from floor to ceiling. Statues of tiefling monks tower overhead. Braziers crackle with flame, casting shadows about the room.

Bent before the largest statue in the centre of the temple, Magician Mittens mutters to himself. His robes pool around him. A book glows green in his paws.

"At last," Mittens says, "with these ancient secrets, I will finally have true power!"

"Not so fast!" Jace strums on his lute. "Drop the book, you bad guy!"

Mittens jumps up with a frightened meow. He extends his claws, tail standing straight up.

"Oh," he says, relaxing. "It's only you."

Ra'ven aims an arrow at the cat. "What a waste of a sneak attack."

"Whoopsie," Jace says.

"We'll work on your Stealth later," Smashwell says.

"We know you lied to us, Mittens," Oakley says. "We don't know why you want that book, but it belongs to somebody else."

"Can anyone own power?" Mittens asks. "The wizarding guild believed so. They cursed me because I dared ask why we should wait for the return of the gods. We have the recipe to make new gods right here! They'll wish they'd turned me into a worm when I find them and crush them like — like worms!"

"You don't need to do this, Mittens," Oakley pleads. "Let us have the book. No one has to get hurt."

"You think I care if I hurt you?" Mittens squeaks. "First I'll crush you. Next I'll crush Pan-Terra!"

"This is hallowed ground," Demonica says. "There will be no crushing today."

Mittens yowls and hunches over. He transforms.

His cries deepen to a lion-like growl. His claws grow bigger and dig into the cracked marble floor. His robes tear as his shoulders widen, muscles bulging beneath his fur. Extra teeth fill his mouth until he can make no expression other than a snarl. Pupils narrowing to sharp black slits, he looks eager to bite the heads off of each of these Silly Geese.

"Now, the final battle begins —!"

Knocking on the doorjamb, Clive peeks his head into the gaming room. "Sorry to interrupt, folks, but it's getting late and I'm gonna start shutting things off and wiping things down. Last call for food or drink."

Hamish froze, posing and baring his teeth like the transforming Mittens.

"One more break," he says, relaxing. "Fuel up. You're gonna need the energy."

13 A Short Rest to Restore Some Hit Points

"MAYBE WE SHOULD HAVE killed those goblins just for the levels," I say as Rumour and I step behind Nathan at the back of the line.

"Wow, Journey," Rumour says, "I didn't know levels were more important to you than goblin lives."

"You know me. All about that grindset."

I regret saying it as soon as the words leave my mouth. She doesn't know me, not really. Even though I'd really like her to. There's no walkthrough to speed-run us to the end of this story. Somehow I'm going to have to keep from putting my foot in my mouth despite being the champion of Saying the Wrong Thing.

"I'm really glad we came tonight," Rumour says.

Heat creeps over my cheeks. "Yeah? I, uh, I told Hamish he'd do great."

"He is. And even though we kinda almost ruined it, Ian's having more fun than he has in ages. School hasn't been easy lately. You know how it can be for queer kids."

Ian and Hamish are both at the counter. Hamish is treating Ian to a second milkshake, with Rumour's permission. I can hear them talking about the unfair cancellation of *The Owl House* from here.

"Is he out?" I ask.

Rumour nods. "We talked about how it might be hard at first. How the world isn't always safe for us. And it doesn't look like it's getting safer any time soon. But there's so much joy in being true to yourself. It doesn't make the bad stuff go away, but it also brings so much good into your life. Real friends who love you for you. Relationships where you don't need to lie about who you are."

"Relationships," I repeat. *Don't say it, don't say it, don't* — "Are you, um, are you in a . . . ?"

No Charisma roll could save someone so hopeless. Even Nathan glances over his shoulder at me and clears his throat before moving to the counter. But Rumour doesn't call me out. She only shakes her head, her ponytail swinging.

"Ah. Cool. Or, uh, not cool if you don't like being, um, being single. But, you know." *Stop. Stop now, you maniac.* "Me neither."

"I really missed you, Journey," she says. "Even though you are super corny."

"I like to think it's a feature, not a bug." I shove my hands into my pockets so they don't do something embarrassing like punch her shoulder or make finger guns. "But I am best friends with my cousin, who has no choice but to love me, so maybe I'm buggier than I know."

"Plenty of people like bugs. Just ask the bug

catchers in every *Pokémon* game, with their little nets and their Caterpies. All trans masc, by the way."

"Of course."

"And lots of people still liked *Fallout: New Vegas.*"

"Deep cut."

"Hey, *New Vegas* is an important part of trans culture. But yes, I'm full of deep cuts. Keeper of ancient nerd lore."

"Are you saying *Fallout: New Vegas* is old? Is that what I'm hearing?" Clive says as we reach the front of the line. "Dear god, I think you're right."

"Sorry to make you aware of the passage of time," Rumour says.

Clive shrugs, pouring Nathan his cup of black coffee. "Nothing your existence doesn't do already. What can I get for you?"

Rumour looks at the counter for a moment, then grins. She grabs the blue d20 and holds it out to me. "Roll with me?"

"I thought you didn't trust your luck," I say.

She shrugs. "Feels like maybe my luck's getting

better."

I take the die from her and roll first. Luck grants me a Lemongrab Loaf. Rumour rolls next and gets a biscotti Thimblet. I also order a standard Haste to go with it because hey, I'm not sleeping tonight anyway.

"You know," Rumour says, "I always really appreciated how kind you were to him. Even when I wasn't. When I couldn't be, because I was wrapped up in my own problems. That part of you hasn't changed, has it? You're still a kind person. You're still . . . you."

"I try to be," I say, but it comes out as barely more than a whisper.

She touches my arm and my entire body lights up like I've been struck by lightning. I clutch my hot mug of espresso to my chest, watching Rumour take her seat. She meets my gaze. I smile. I don't look away.

A sun burns in the middle of my chest, hot and bright and life-giving. It's a feeling I recognize. A feeling that used to burn in me all the time. It makes me think of grade eight, when Rumour and I played through *Breath of the Wild*, fingers brushing as we passed the Switch back and forth. Of holding hands tobogganing down the big hill at Centennial Park. Of all the sleepovers we had, wrapped up in the same comforter, staying up way too late watching scary movies.

It feels like she was never gone.

Once I sit down, Nathan straightens to his full height, puffing out the chest of his cardigan with a long inhale. He drums lightly on the tabletop. He exhales through whistling nostrils.

"I apologize," he blurts out.

We wait for him to say something else.

When it's clear he needs a little help, Greta prompts him. "For?"

"For my . . . behaviour."

"Which behaviour and directed at *whom*?" Greta says.

Nathan's head swivels on his neck like a robot locking onto his target. "Ian. Jace the bloody Bard. I have not been very welcoming to you. I . . . am stuck in my ways, sometimes. Change makes me feel . . . weird. Scratchy. Uncomfortable. Because of that, I'm not always as fun to be around as I would like. But I know if there had been a cranky jerk like me in my first campaign, I might never have continued playing *Dungeons & Dragons*. I'd be a carpenter or a prima ballerina instead of a hopeless nerd, and I would be miserable. I don't want to ruin this for you. So I am sorry."

"Wow, I didn't even tell him to say most of that," Greta says. "That came from the heart."

"Proof he has one," Hamish says.

"It's okay, Nathan," Ian says. "The Silliest Geese stick together."

"Yes," Nathan says. "They do."

I pump my fist. "To the Silliest Geese!"

Almost everyone matches my enthusiasm, banging the table and chanting, "Silliest Geese! Silliest Geese!"

"Honk," Nathan deadpans.

14 Cue Boss Battle Music

"SO LET ME GET THIS STRAIGHT," Nathan says when everyone settles down. "First you steal the name of their deceased cat for an NPC."

"In my defence, I didn't know he was dead!" Hamish says.

"And now you want them to murder their deceased cat."

"As an *artiste*, I simply let the story flow through me." Hamish puts one hand to his temple and holds the other out like he's searching for a story. Like Professor X reading minds, plagiarizing books with the power of Cerebro.

"Hamish," Greta says.

He opens one eye, aims it at Ian and Rumour. "Sorry again."

"Nah, I don't mind," Ian says.

"Transforming into a powerful monster is exactly what Mittens would have wanted," Rumour says. "He had a mean streak. I've got the ankle scars to prove it."

"Then perhaps it is his spirit that flows through our story this day!" Hamish again makes a pose like he's summoning the dead at a seance.

Because an important part of being deputy to the DM is nagging people when it's 11:21 p.m., I say, "It's getting pretty late."

"All right, all right, Hamish gets the point." Hamish taps his phone. Latin choral chanting begins. "Who's ready to fight a boss battle?"

"We're gonna die for sure," Rumour says.

Magician Mittens's giant shoulders nudge architecture out of the way, showering the party in dust, stone, and splinters of wood. Standing in his shadow, even those without Detect Magic can feel his power, along with a wave of overwhelming fear. But the party holds their ground.

In a voice so deep it shakes everyone's eardrums, Mittens says, "Still think I'm cute?"

"Extremely!" Smashwell says.

"Well, stop it!"

"There's more of you to love!"

Attacking first, Demonica grips her staff. She plants her feet and shouts, "Magic missile!"

The darts of magic energy split into three paths. They explode against Mittens's snout, neck, and chest. "That tickles."

"I guess this super villain isn't worried about sounding unoriginal," Ra'ven says.

The giant cat swipes his massive paw downward,

crashing through a column. Demonica leaps out of the way. The strike slams into the floor right where she'd stood, leaving a deep paw print. A chunk of column crashes into Smashwell, pinning her against the wall. Jace summons his Magic Hand to free Smashwell —

"Nobody yell at me," Nathan says, "but —"

Like a bullying hive mind, we all start yelling at him.

"Mage Hand can't carry more than ten pounds!"

Our shouting turns into booing.

"I'm not saying I have a problem with bending the rules!" Nathan says. "I'm just making sure we're bending them intentionally!"

Hamish rises from behind his partition. "Okay, okay. All in favour of giving Jace a special ability called Jace's Hand, which can carry varying weight depending on an Intelligence check."

Everyone says, "Aye!" Even Nathan.

"Do I get a special rule-breaking move?" he asks.

"Are you twelve?" Hamish says.

"It's up for debate," Greta says.

"Just thought I'd ask," Nathan says.

After freeing Smashwell, Jace sets Kai in the palm of his Jace Hand. "A battle is no place for my beautiful baby boy. Stay hidden."

The hand flies up to the ceiling and tucks Kai into a crack in the wall.

"Hit him with your magic hand!" Demonica shouts.

"He can't," Ra'ven says as he releases an arrow and front-flips out of the way of another swipe. Somehow without landing on his face! "It's still non-offensive!"

But the hand had already curled into a fist. See-through purple knuckles rocket toward Mittens, cracking into the cat's nose. Mittens only growls, unmoving.

"That doesn't make any sense!" Demonica says.

"I don't make the rules!" Ra'ven says.

Mittens cackles, his booming laughter echoing throughout the temple. "I MAKE THE RULES! I AM YOUR GOD!"

"I have an idea!" Oakley cries, jumping in front of Smashwell. "Throw me!"

The half-orc lifts Oakley, spins around twice, and launches the blade-wielding halfling through the dusty air. The edge of their short sword slices into fur and severs a whisker, which plummets to the ground as if made of steel. The whisker jabs needle-like into the floor.

Mittens shakes his massive head. "That tickles also. I! Am! Very! TICKLISH!"

"Stop tickling the kaiju!" Ra'ven shouts.

Before Oakley can fall, Mittens hits the halfling out of the air. Oakley crashes to the ground with a sickening crack.

Smashwell gasps.

"Oh no!" Jace cries.

Blood trickles from Oakley's forehead. No breath passes their lips. Not even their heartbeat thuds against Demonica's fingers.

"Oh my gods," the tiefling whispers. "Don't die on me. You're not allowed. We only just — just became friends. Wake up, Oakley!"

But Oakley does not respond.

"What the shit, Journey?" Rumour says.

"Hey, the move works for Wolverine!" I say with a shrug that does not match how embarrassed I am for dying *immediately*. I had hoped the move would do more damage. Or at least look cooler. Hamish is just laughing at me and narrating my demise like a bad *D&D* wingman.

"You know why? Healing factor, you goober!"

And I don't know what it is about her yelling at me, but I'm blushing and it's not out of embarrassment.

"Should we start rolling death saves?" Hamish asks with that goofy grin of his. "Three chances. Ten or higher and Oakley stabilizes."

"Hey, it's not even my turn!" I cry. "Anyone wanna heal me?"

"It wouldn't be a final battle without a heroic sacrifice," Greta says with a sigh. Then she winks at me. "But I guess I can spare a spell. I move two squares to the right, touch Oakley, and use Spare the Dying.

Who wants this scarf?"

"I do!" Ian says, jumping up and snatching the red and green scarf held out to him. "Thank you, it's *super* soft."

While Ian's rubbing the scarf on his face, Nathan's looking over my shoulder. "Make sure you use Second Wind," he says, completely taking the Second Wind from my sails.

To a chorus of agreements, I say, "I was going to make you wait for it, for *the drama*, but fine. I use Second Wind, stand up with gritted teeth" — I put up my fists like a boxer — "and say, 'I can do this all day.'"

"Nice," Nathan approves with a nod.

"And then I say, 'Wait, did Demonica really say we're friends?'"

Rumour smirks, shaking her head. "'Don't get too excited, little fighter. We still have a god to kill.'"

Still blushing, I roll my d10. "Nine plus my fighter level — Second Wind gives me back ten hit points. We won't be doing that move again, though, just to be clear. I don't have a Third Wind. Ian's turn."

Ian bounces in his seat and shouts, "My Jace Hand skids to a stop behind you guys like that move motorcycles do in anime."

"You better not know which anime," Rumour says.

"All this dust puffs up in the air and Jace says, 'Hold on to your butts! I'm gonna cast Thunderwave!'"

"Will you sing, though?" Nathan says.

"Hey, we talked about this," Rumour says. "He doesn't have to —"

"Yes." Ian stands up. He clasps his hands in front of him, but not before I notice them shaking. "I'll do it."

"No one is forcing you," I say. "It doesn't matter what Nathan thinks —"

"Agree to disagree," Nathan grumbles.

"Disagree to agree," Greta says.

"That doesn't mean anything," he says.

"Agree to disagree," she says.

"We already voted," I say. "No one has to do anything that makes them uncomfortable."

Nathan rolls his eyes. "I'm not trying to make him uncomfortable. I'm just saying, if the kid wants to sing, I bet we'd all find the power of music stat-boosting. With the Dungeon Master's permission, of course."

"I can feel you playing all of us," Hamish says. "But you're right. This Dungeon Master would be impressed by the bravery and everyone would get superpowers."

"Guys, I already said I'd do it!" Ian says.

He straightens his posture. He takes a big breath.

And then he *sings*.

The lyrics are, admittedly, pretty silly. He rhymes "giant cat" with "how 'bout that?" But his voice transforms completely, shoving the awkward, shy Ian out of the way. He belts out vocals that belong on *America's Got Talent* (or one of those other shows where a mean Simon Cowell-type tells Ian he made his heart grow three sizes bigger).

"Oh my god," Hamish whispers, actual for-real

tears pouring down his face. He brings his hands together in a strong, solid clap, and the rest of us join in. "That was *gorgeous*."

Ian smiles and puts his hands behind his head. "Yeah?"

"One hundred percent. Stat boosts for everyone. You're all Super Saiyan now. And the Thunderwave sends a burning electrical current through Mittens's colossal form. His body jerks and he makes cartoony electrocution sounds." Hamish demonstrates by shaking his whole body, making a wobbly high-pitched noise and rattling his teeth. "Then he collapses against the biggest of the tiefling statues, stunned."

"Yes!" Nathan growls, slamming a palm on the table. The mini-figures bounce. "What did I tell you, kid? We can't waste this boost. What's our plan?"

Greta looks up from her knitting, where she's already started a second project. "Is that the spirit of collaboration I hear, babe? Are you growing up?"

"Hush, you," he says, gently elbowing her.

"I might have an idea," Rumour says, leaning

toward me. "Hey, Journey, how about we try the Sole Orb Special?"

"Like, *King of Coats*?" I ask. "Of park roleplay fame?"

"The very same. I think with Witch Bolt and Ian's stat boosts, we can recreate the scene with Grunklehorn the Giant and destroy this bastard."

"Classic scene," Nathan says.

"We'll distract him," Ian says. Picking at a loose string in his cloak, his eyes widen. "I pull a loose string out of my cloak. I use my Unseen Servant to dangle it in front of Mittens."

The long string floats in front of the giant cat, flying past his nose. Mittens's eyes grow wide and round. He swipes at the string.

While he's distracted, Smashwell tosses a handful of sand from her pocket. The grains of sand hum with magical energy before exploding like popcorn into a wave of water. The water coats the floor. Mittens yowls, hopping from one foot to the other, splashing water everywhere.

An arrow strikes Mittens's chin.

"What can you possibly hope to gain from this foolishness?" Mittens growls. "Do you plan to insult me to death? I am no house cat! I am not afraid of water!"

"You do seem kind of afraid of water," Demonica says.

"I'm not!" Mittens says, still hopping. "I'm powerful!"

Sparking blue energy stretches between Demonica's palms. Her boots scuff against stone as she plants her feet wide. She lashes out with the crackling Witch Bolt, connecting herself to Mittens and shocking the giant cat once more. Thanks to the water, the electrocution damage doubles.

Another arrow jams between Mittens's eyes. Mittens snaps the arrow shaft in half with a swat of his paw and opens his mouth. From the back of his throat rises a bright white glow, along with a loud humming sound. Clawing into the sculpted face of the closest statue, Mittens lifts it onto his shoulder.

Twisting his body, he sends the statue flying toward Demonica.

She has no choice but to jump out of the way. The Witch Bolt blinks into nothingness.

"You cannot defeat me! All of Pan-Terra will bow to me!" The giant cat cackles. The light in his throat shines even brighter. "None of you shall survive my special move: Ultima Beam Breath!"

Suddenly, his laughter stops. "Wait. Where is the little one —?"

Oakley had been, during this time, scaling the temple wall. Their arms trembled with fear and exhaustion. Their toes slipped from unsteady holds. Their fingers threatened to give up on them. But they reached the top of the wall, gave Kai a quick ruffle of his curly hair, and drew their sword.

Then, when Mittens began bragging about his unlimited power, Oakley leapt. They held their sword point-down and let gravity do the rest.

Mittens mutters, "— I swear I just saw them, gotta be around here somewhere —"

Oakley's sword sinks to the hilt. Buried in Mittens's skull.

The giant staggers. The light in his throat fades. "I . . . I was going to return it," he mumbles, reaching for the walls to steady himself. "To seal it away. But its power . . . What I could do with such power . . ."

He drops to his knees, then falls onto his face with a crash that shakes the temple. Oakley is thrown from their hold atop the cat's skull. Smashwell catches them out of the air.

"Told you guys I was a monster slayer," Oakley says.

15 Books and Their Covers

EVERYONE AT THE TABLE whoops and cheers. I'm out of my seat before I can talk myself down, and I'm wrapping my arms around Rumour. The warmth of her body presses against my chest, heats my arms. She smells like cardamom and cinnamon, a walking pumpkin spice latte. She feels soft and sweet and *right*. A missing piece of my life that, now I've found her again, I'm afraid to let go.

Over Rumour's shoulder, I catch Hamish

grinning at me. It's what makes me realize we've held each other a moment too long. I let go like Rumour's a burning baking sheet and I've forgotten my oven mitts. I take off my hat to scratch my head, put my hat back on, and take way too long to sit back down.

"Everyone levels up," Hamish says. "Incredible work, Silliest Geese."

"I loot Mittens's giant furry body," Rumour says.

"While he's still warm," I say.

"I'm not here to waste time."

Hamish says, "You find a scuffed crystal ball, fifty gold pieces, and a leather notebook, no longer glowing."

Rumour's face lights up. "I almost forgot we were looking for this stupid book! Is this it? Did we finish the quest?"

"Well, Demonica now holds the ancient, powerful book that drove Mittens to seek revenge and godhood. She feels its pull. She hears its whispered promises. Wouldn't she like revenge for what was done to her people? Rumour, roll a Constitution check."

"Shit," Rumour says. "What happens if I fail?"

"Then your party might have another boss fight to deal with."

"No pressure." Rumour takes a deep breath. Her face sets into an expression of determination I can't look away from. She takes her d20 and shakes it in both hands.

She lets go. The die bounces, rolls, and stops.

I cry out, "Nat twenty!"

The crowd, once again, goes wild.

"How do you feel?" Oakley asks Demonica, hand on her elbow.

Holding up the book and flipping through the pages, Demonica says, "I've got it under control. Weird that this little book is so powerful, though. It does basically look like a cookbook. It even has whole diary entries before each recipe."

"Hate that," Oakley says. "We don't need to know about how you found yourself on unicorn-back with the love of your life who won't call you anymore. I just want to know how long to cook my rice so it doesn't get soggy or burnt. What do we do with it?"

"Don't we give it back to Master Petrin?" Jace says.

Above him, his Jace Hand pinches the collar of Kai's tunic and carries the goblin child gently to Jace's arms. But Kai wiggles and slides to the floor, wandering away.

"I don't like the idea of banning books," Smashwell says, clutching her own book to her chest, "but this might be the exception."

"It's obviously dangerous," Demonica says. "Petrin didn't tell us the truth."

"Maybe he had a good reason to lie to us," Ra'ven says. "We could have turned out as power hungry as Mittens."

"Uh, guys?" Jace says from deeper inside the temple, following Kai. "There's stuff back here."

Behind the collapsed main statue and its altar, treasure chests fill a circular room. Thumb in his mouth,

Kai heads for one of the chests. Jace grabs his hand and redirects him back to the party.

"Why would there be a treasure room inside a temple?" Oakley says.

"How long has it been abandoned?" Demonica asks. "Wait, I should know that, obviously. It's been years since the assaults on our religion. Who knows how many bandits may have used this place since?"

"It's a trap," Ra'ven says. "I know it is. Those are all mimics. This is a mimic nest."

"Don't mimics hunt alone?" Oakley asks.

"Doesn't matter. They'll break any rule to feast on my flesh."

"You know," Smashwell says, "if you'd made mimics your preferred enemy instead of goblins, I think you'd have a much easier time."

Oakley picks a chest at random, right in the middle of the row. "I'm taking the chance."

"But your health is so low!" Jace says.

"Live a little," Oakley says. "You in?"

Demonica stands before the chest to their left. "YOLO."

"What the hell," Smashwell says, choosing the one to Oakley's right. "We took out a giant magical cat. What's a treasure chest with teeth?"

"Stay here," Jace tells Kai. He sets the goblin child down outside the room, on the fluffy chair-sized paw of the giant cat in question. "Okay, on three."

"You're all insane." Ra'ven holds his bow and his last arrow nervously, waiting in the doorway.

"Three," Smashwell says.

"Two," says Demonica.

"ONE!" Oakley shouts.

The four adventurers each unlatch a chest. They open with a crack of old leather and a creak of dry wood. Inside are piles of gold pieces, gemstones, magical rings and scrolls, potions of healing, and a black dagger.

"Come on, babe," Smashwell says, "just pick a chest, get some treasure. You don't want to miss out."

Ra'ven hesitates, shifting his weight from foot to foot. He clearly wants the treasure. He hungers to be proven wrong. His hands shake with the strength of holding himself back. The fear of missing out is simply too great for him. He must touch the treasure.

"Fine!" He beelines to the chest beside Smashwell. He kicks it once. The chest rattles, settles, and stays put. Slowly, Ra'ven crouches and places a hand on either side of the lid. He looks at the rest of the party as they empty their treasure into Demonica's bag of holding.

Ra'ven opens the chest.

The chest lunges at him. Rows of pointed teeth line the rectangular opening of the mimic's mouth. A tongue of leather licks his nose. Ra'ven screams as heavy copper pieces spill painfully onto his face —

"You can't do that!" Nathan says.

"Do what?" Hamish squeaks, wiping tears from his eyes.

"Make my chest a mimic!"

I'm laughing so hard I struggle to breathe, my eyes bleary and watery. Though there's still a distracted part of me that focuses on Rumour's giggle and the way it tosses my heart into a kiln.

"Swear to every god in the *Player's Handbook*, I changed none of my plans. Look." Hamish passes over a sheet of paper where he's drawn a messy blueprint of the treasure room. Each of the chests are labelled. "This is pure luck."

Nathan tosses the paper onto the grid, knocking over the miniatures. "Unbelievable."

In between chuckles, Greta says, "I grab the mimic by both ends and try to rip it in half. Is an opposed Athletics check okay?"

"Go for it," Hamish says with great difficulty.

She rolls, cheeks rosy. Hamish rolls, too. Greta gets the higher Athletics score.

"Splinters rain over Ra'ven. The two halves of the mimic hit opposite walls," Hamish says.

"There, babe. You're safe now."

Leaning his head all the way down to her shoulder, Nathan says, "My hero."

"Are there any other rooms?" Rumour says. "Wait, let me guess: that's an Investigation check."

"You're getting the hang of it," I say. "Hamish would say he's proud if he could stop giggling for five seconds."

"Too true," Hamish says. Greta gets a seventeen and he confirms, "That's all there is to this temple."

"Good. It is way past a certain ten-year-old's bedtime."

"Awww," Ian says, though he's resting his chin on the back of his hands like he could fall asleep any second.

"Gotta have those long rests to regain your spell slots," I tell him.

"Jace also doesn't like bedtimes. It's canon now. He and Kai will party all night and there's nothing you can do about it."

"Sure, sure, buddy," Rumour says. "Time to decide what we're going to do with this book."

Nathan tents his fingers under his chin. "There is a theme here. Don't judge a book by its cover. The cute cat was a villain. The goblins were kind and reasonable. Even the chef at The Silly Goose wasn't the good guy we were supposed to think he was."

"Did we help the bad guy?" Ian asks.

"*A* bad guy, maybe not *the* bad guy," Rumour says. "The crabs did say they wanted revenge for what the chef did on their island. He's a total colonizer."

"Darn it," Ian whispers. "I totally boiled those guys to death."

"If I know anything about Hamish's weak-willed view of the world," Nathan says, "I bet he made Petrin sketchy to trick us. Hamish wanted us to think he was evil. There's even a good chance Petrin cursed Mittens himself, to tie it all together."

"Metagamey as all heck, man," Hamish says.

"Whatever. I say we give the creepy old man his book."

The Silly Goose hasn't recovered from the revenge of the Clawbertons. With most of the furniture broken, the tavern's patrons lean on walls, or sit on wooden crates. The music and conversation can be heard from the town's borders, as the windows have yet to be repaired. A bucket sits on the counter, and a note beside it reads, PLEEZE TIPPE 4 RE-PARES.

Master Petrin is sipping an ale when the Silliest Geese enter the tavern, dirt-streaked and exhausted. A single black feather sits behind his ear.

Ra'ven is the first to sit at the table while the rest of the party drag over their own crates. He slaps the cookbook on the tabletop. "You lied to us."

"I apologize for misleading you, but I did not know who to trust," the old man says. "The magic between the lines of these recipes are older than the gods. You will get your gold, as promised."

Master Petrin places a heavy sack of rattling gold coins on the counter.

Ra'ven opens the bag and sifts through it, taking out a gold coin and biting down on it. But when Petrin reaches for the book, Ra'ven pulls it away. "I think a tip might help us forgive the lack of honesty."

"I was about to suggest the same," Petrin says, handing over another, smaller bag.

Ra'ven hands both sacks of gold to Demonica. She puts them into her bag of holding.

"Pleasure doing business," Ra'ven says.

Master Petrin stashes the cookbook inside a coat pocket and stands. "Thank you dearly, brave adventurers. Without you, I know not what I would have done with my remaining years. Times being what they are, there are few job opportunities for the Dark Emperor's fallen angels."

Great black wings unfurl from Master Petrin's back.

"Shit," Ra'ven says.

"Not again!" cries Chef Laios as he ducks behind the counter.

"But he was never much of an Emperor anyway. I'll do what he couldn't." Master Petrin smiles too wide. His skin reddens, dark as blood. Horns pierce the flesh of his forehead as they grow, and rise, and curl. "What happens to Pan-Terra when I plunge the realm into darkness is because of your efforts."

Everyone at the table jumps to their feet. Jace covers Kai with his body and turns away from the fallen angel.

Smashwell flips a table and holds it as a shield in front of the party. Ra'ven aims an arrow. His arrow flies true, hitting exactly where Master Petrin's heart would be —

Too slow. Petrin's giant wings wrap around his body, covering himself completely. Feathers cloud the tavern common room. With a whoosh, the fallen angel is gone.

"Well," Oakley says, "that could have gone better."

And with a snap of his closing notebook, Hamish says, "To be continued . . ."

Everyone around the table groans.

16 You, Me, and D&D

"WAIT A MINUTE!" Ian says. "There weren't any dungeons *or* dragons."

"Gotta leave them wanting more," Hamish says while he packs up, folding his privacy screen. "I really can't believe you gave Petrin his book back. Dude was obviously evil. It was so hard not to laugh at you trying to outsmart me."

"This whole game has ruined my childhood," Nathan says.

"You're finally a grown-up, then," Greta says, hooking her arm around his elbow.

"You loved it," Hamish says. "Kept you on your toes."

"Yeah," Nathan says with a shrug. "It was fun."

"The nicest compliment you've ever given me!" Hamish says. "I'll take it, deposit it in the bank, and watch it gain interest."

"This is why I don't compliment you." Nathan tips his head back and drains the rest of his coffee.

"No take-backs. And hey, I wanted to thank you."

"For?"

"For being my rules guy."

Nathan pauses with the mug against his lips, an eyebrow arched. "Really?"

"Yeah, man. I know it gets annoying when I break most of the rules anyway, but I need you when I legit don't know what I'm talking about."

"Oh. Well." Nathan blinks slowly. He might be malfunctioning. "I appreciate you saying that."

Backpack in hand, Ian jumps beside Nathan. "See you again next week?"

Nathan in his six-foot-five-ness looms over Ian and nods. "I look forward to the next chapter."

Ian gives him a huge smile. Rumour pulls Ian aside, helping him pack up his things.

"Hamish, we'll be in the car," Greta says. She and Nathan shout their goodbyes to the rest of us from the front door, then brave the snow.

Hamish doesn't take long. He slings his bag over his shoulder, and he punches my arm.

"Ow?" I say.

"You're welcome," he says.

"For the bruise?"

He shakes his head and steps outside.

Rumour and Ian's dad pulls up to the curb in a white SUV. He honks the horn.

"Go ahead," Rumour says to her brother, fingernails tapping her earlobe. "I think I lost an earring."

"Do you want help?" Ian asks.

"Nah, tell Dad I'll be a sec."

Before he leaves, Ian turns on his heel and jumps at me with open arms. I laugh and hug him back. "Thanks, Journey," is all he says before rushing out to the car.

Grinning to myself, I say to Rumour, "I can help look, just let me grab my stuff from the back first."

I bring my armful of *D&D* stuff to the cramped staff room and dump everything into my backpack. I can't believe it's midnight already. The night went by so quickly.

I'm not ready for it to be over.

A flash of pink bounces in the corner of my eye. Rumour's rocking on her heels in the doorway and smiling in a way that immediately makes me blush. It's so different from the look she gave me when she first walked in. When it looked like her life was flashing before her eyes.

What flashes before us now is limitless future. Infinite possibilities. A whole new timeline unlocked.

"Oh," I say, very suave, very cool. "Uh, h-hey there. Um. Hi."

"Hi."

Rumour bites her lip, and I have to look down at my open backpack before my head explodes. She nudges the break room door closed.

"That was really great," I say. "When you told us Demonica's mysterious past, I was speechless. You're . . . You're amazing."

"That was only the beginning of my secret backstory. There's so much more to tell."

"Hey, you can't tease me when the game's over."

"Call it foreshadowing. To make sure you show up next time."

"That's not fair."

"Isn't it?" She takes a single step into the room. A single step closer to me. "Maybe I can tell you, but you'll have to keep it a secret."

She stops with mere inches left between us. Her pumpkin spice scent. I meet her eyes, rich brown with waves of gold, like a tiger's eye crystal, searching mine.

"I'm great at keeping secrets," I say. "Mostly because I don't have anyone to tell."

Another step. Her coat brushes my waistcoat.

"Demonica first encountered magic during prayer," she says. "She was unhappy but couldn't put it into words. She asked for a sign from the Chimera, to guide her. Her eyes fell on a girl her age, on the colours she was allowed to wear, the bows in her hair. Demonica understood. And when she was sure of what she needed, she told her friend, her *best* friend, that she wasn't a boy after all. That she'd always been a girl. But her friend was scared. They ran away from her."

I say nothing, because I asked for this. Because I deserve it. I only hold her gaze, staying here with her now even though it hurts. My mouth is dry. Her palm presses against my chest, where my heart sends ripples of apology to her fingertips.

"Demonica grew up to become a wizard, seeking to learn everything about magic. She used this magic the way the Chimera taught, to become more of who she was on the inside. She made for herself a life where she could finally show everyone her true power. The true power of all the girls like her, who could find happiness if they follow their hearts. And she was happy, most of the time. But something was missing. She found that missing piece, that missing person, one winter evening in a nerdy café."

There's a moment of tension, one that could easily slip away from us with nothing said. A night that could become just like any other.

I won't let that happen.

"There's another reason I was scared. Before. When we were still friends," I say.

"Tell me."

My hands tremble. I can't catch my breath. "I always had a crush on you. For as long as I knew what a crush was. I know it's weird."

"I don't think it's weird . . ."

"I didn't think I was allowed to feel that way about my best friend. And I really didn't think I could *ever* tell you. You had too much to worry about. And then, after I — after I ran away, and we were still in classes together where I could watch you become stronger, and braver, and more . . . more beautiful. More yourself. It was really hard. Thinking we'd never be friends again. Lov — uh, having a, um, a crush on you. I never stopped wondering, what if?"

"What if what?" she whispers, closer still. Her mouth so near I can feel the words on my skin.

"What if I'd been there for you? What if I was braver?"

"It's never too late to be brave."

"Do you — do you want to go on a date sometime?" I cringe as soon as I say it. "Maybe it's too soon. We only just repaired our friendship but I —"

"Do you want to kiss me?"

I nod, holding her hands, keeping them against my chest.

Her shoes bump mine. I barely need to lower my head. Her lips part, soft and inviting. I sink into her, drawn to the heat of her mouth like a moth to a flame. I release her hands and hold her cheeks. Never wanting to let go. Her hands find their way under my shirt, frost-tipped and sharp-nailed on my hips. She pulls me even closer until there's no room left between us at all — and I ache to be closer still.

A car horn honks a second time. I jump, taking a step back. But she pulls me back into her orbit, holds me close like the Earth must hold the moon. We stand there in our embrace until our heavy breathing slows.

"Yes, Journey. I would love to go on a date."

Rumour grabs my face and kisses me one more time before pulling away and opening the door to the break room. I hold her hand until her fingers slip from mine, out of reach.

"So there'll be a next time?" I ask. "Is that a promise?"

"There'll be tomorrow at school, you dingus."

"Right. Obviously." I take off my toque, sweeping back my bangs. "For a second there, I forgot anything but you, me, and *D&D* even existed."

She smiles at me, just for me, and hurries outside. I watch her jump inside the car. And then she's gone.

I grab my things. Clive is sitting at a table by the front window, swiping on his phone.

“Ready to go,” I say.

We step into the piling snow. Keys jingling in his gloved hand, Clive locks the door to Limited Series.

“Well, I hope you kids had a fun time,” Clive says. “Good night.”

“Great night,” I say, my breath a cloud streaming from my tingling lips.

I walk home, barely feeling the cold.

EPILOGUE
Return of the King of Coats

AFTER TWO MONTHS of Ian's begging, Nathan finally failed his Constitution roll. He had no choice but to meet us at Limited Series and suffer through a *King of Coats: Pockets of Peace* marathon.

Tonight's the season finale, and somehow we've gotten him not to leave despite many threats that he would. I'm pressed up on the end of the couch, my left elbow on the arm rest and my right arm wrapped around Rumour like if I let go even for a second a high wind might blow her away. Ian snuggles close on her other side.

"I still don't think Zephyr would *ever* give up the Ultima Coat just because that kid might one day be king," Nathan complains from the middle cushion of the beat-up couch. "It could be a self-fulfilling prophecy, and then Zephyr causes the total downfall of the kingdom by trusting some orphan peasant. Why not take the throne himself?"

"It makes perfect sense if you think about the *themes*," Greta says, perched over him on the other arm rest. "*King of Coats* has always been about honour and how true power is found in generosity and kindness."

"But he knows he's marching to his death! How will he defeat the Blacksuit Brigade now? Why not wait until after defeating Tuxevo?"

"Dude," Hamish says from a pink beanbag on the floor, "Tuxevo could take the Ultima Coat for himself, and then there would be no kingdom to be king of."

Clive places a platter of Triforce appetizers and a

Cheese Wheel of Time on the coffee table.

"Fresh out of the oven," he says, pulling over a chair and sitting on it backward like a teacher trying too hard to be cool. "What did I miss?"

"A lot of arguing," I say.

"Nathan trying really hard not to admit he likes the show," Rumour says.

"The word 'admit' is doing a lot of heavy lifting," Nathan says.

"Come on. Give the show a single compliment," she says. "For Ian, the once and future king."

Ian, for his part, pouts and bats his long eyelashes. Weaponized cuteness at its most dangerous.

Nathan sighs. "The camera work is almost on par with the original trilogy. It's very . . ." He struggles with the end of his sentence. ". . . pretty."

"You're getting soft, old man," Greta says, planting a kiss in his beard.

"I'm twenty-two."

"I said what I said."

On the screen, the three-piece-suit-wearing Zephyr

Morningblade dons his Cufflinks of Clarity and raises his broadsword. At his side stands Princess Cassandra in her tattered white wedding dress and the dragon-blessed Veil of Valour. She draws an arrow, the arrowhead crackling with the golden energy of her light magic.

Black fog blankets the once green plains of the battlefield. With a screeching battle cry, Tuxevo's horde of the bespoke undead rush forth from the open gates of the Blacksuit Fortress.

Rumour taps me with one green acrylic nail. Between the tense finale of my favourite television series and my girlfriend needing my attention, it's an easy choice.

Girlfriend. I'll never get tired of that.

I turn and kiss her right between her perfect eyebrows. She scrunches up her face, her lips green with lipstick matching her nails, and I plant another kiss on the tip of her nose.

My whole body is warm and tingly. My health metre is not only full but has extra hit points, shining and golden. We haven't said The Words yet, but I feel them raging through me. I can't stop fantasizing about the perfect moment to tell Rumour I'm in love with her. Not that it should come as a surprise.

I've always been in love with her.

Maybe I'll tell her later tonight.

Until then, we fall into our usual lines, what feels like a placeholder for the final step. "I'm happy," she whispers in my ear.

Pressing my forehead to hers, I whisper, "Me too."

ACKNOWLEDGEMENTS

This book would not exist without Allister Thompson, acquisitions editor at Lorimer. My thanks go to him, Morgan Wright, Megan Kearns, Hanna Caunda, and James Lorimer.

Infinite thanks to Miranda Moth, my number one first reader for life, and the original Demonica.

Thanks to Bob, the original Ra'ven, who loaned me a 30lbs bag of *D&D* books.

To Toby, who will know why.

To Bones McKay, for beta-reading an early draft and saying it was "Bazinga (complimentary)" (among other helpful advice).

To Lisa Asanuma and Lisa Para, for their input on my pitch. Extra thanks to Lisa Para for gifting me "Better ChocoLate Than Never."

Thanks to Maya Ameyaw, Vanessa Ricci-Thode, Marion Lougheed, and Markus Harwood-Jones, for their support and advice as I navigated the weirdness of being approached by a publisher.

Extra production-related thanks to Vivi Partridge and Kate Phillips, whose artworks make this book so much cooler.

The creation of this work was funded in part by the Ontario Arts Council grant. Thanks, provincial funding!

Thanks to every queer person in my life. Like Journey, I was once a scared, repressed 12-year-old. I was unkind to queer friends who needed me before I was ready. I'm lucky I had the room to grow and the community to support me in my own journey, and that I can pass on stories of queer kids finding love, happiness, and community of their own.

And thank you, for reading my book.

THE LIMITED SERIES GAME SESSION

HAMISH'S NOTE TO SELF

Things to remember for a first-time DM (it's totally going to be great, you got this, Future Hamish! *Thanks, Past Hamish!!*):

- 1 round is 6 seconds
- movement is the Speed stat, 1 square of grid paper takes 5 movement speed
- proficiency bonus for level 1 is +2
- spell slots is the number of spells you can use before a rest can refill them, NOT the number of spells the caster knows
- level and class level are not the same
- improv rules! "Yes, AND" to as much player input as possible!
- remember: the most important thing is everyone has fun!

ABILITY SCORES MECHANICS

Ability Score	Modifier
1	-5
2-3	-4
4-5	-3
6-7	-2
8-9	-1
10-11	0
12-13	+1
14-15	+2
16-17	+3

THE HISTORY OF PAN-TERRA

The world of Pan-Terra was, until very recently, like early Greek mythology. Gods just walked around and did stuff with the people they created. They advised kings. Praying to them gave real powers, and displeasing them gave real bad consequences. But then the War of the Gods pitted them and their followers against each other. What gods survived went into hiding, leaving Pan-Terra a land abandoned by its creators — and leaving a god-sized power vacuum . . .

LOCATIONS AND CHARACTERS OVERVIEW

THE SILLY GOOSE

A tavern for adventurers. See description and history on the next page. We start here and I'll have Master Petrin give everyone their first quest, so we get started quickly.

Characters in The Silly Goose

Chef Laios: The owner and head chef of The Silly Goose. A former famous adventurer who is now retired, having followed his dreams of opening a mid-tier restaurant. (Clive's old player character! But is he an alternate dimension version, or did the same guy stumble into Pan-Terra?)

Master Petrin: An old man with a lifetime of secrets and a quest to give. He's misplaced a very valuable recipe book during his last visit to the Temple of the

Chimera, and he's got the bags of gold to hire anyone willing to retrieve it for him.

Tavern patrons: Random NPCs who matter less, but who player characters will definitely want to know about. A boy barbarian . . . baker? A dwarf girl ready to date again. An old gnome with deep pockets, searching for the next musical sensation. Various human adventurers. And a goblin sous chef who secretly works in the back.

The Clawbertons: Our first enemy encounter! A group of crab-men come to take revenge on Chef Laios.

THE ROAD

The main road. A great spot to meet travellers, monsters, or bandits.

Characters Found on the Road

The Traveller: A halfling wizard heads down the road, offering a side quest. He brings word of a goblin colony squatting in the mines.

Bandits: A possible second encounter, but only if the players resist going to the goblins. Standard issue bandits.

THE GOBLIN HORDE WITHIN THE DWARVEN MINES

Once upon a time, the dwarves carved deep mines into human land. But they mined too deep and the Emperor of Darkness used their tunnels to send his army to the mortal plane. The goblins moved in shortly after the Emperor was defeated. The bad history of the place keeps the goblins safe from outsiders.

Characters Found in the Dwarven Mines

The Goblin King: The leader of the goblin colony. A good and just leader. If he reasons with the players, he will set them back on their path. If the players want a fight, well . . . good luck.

The goblin colony: Assorted goblin NPCs. Just normal people with normal jobs, including guards to keep danger out of the mines.

THE TEMPLE OF THE CHIMERA

An abandoned temple to a fallen god. Inside, the players will find a recipe book that's more than I've let on, and a Final Boss who wants its power.

Once the final boss has been battled, the players need a reward — if they don't die, anyway. In a treasure room, there will be as many chests as there are players. One of them has a special surprise . . .

CHARACTER SHEETS

Oakley Goldenrod

LEVEL 1

Played by: **Journey**

APPEARANCE: Taller than the average halfling. They have shaggy brown hair and big brown eyes. Also a small scar on their neck that they say is from a close call with a vampire but is really from an angry turkey. Their favourite colour is red, and it shows in their clothing choices.

BACKSTORY: It's hard making friends when you're different, especially in a halfling community. At 3'6", Oakley stood out in a halfling crowd even before they changed their pronouns or developed a passion for monster-slaying. The choice to leave wasn't an easy one to make, but Oakley finally started their adventure a year ago. They've been a freelance monster hunter ever since.

HALFLING TRAITS: Lucky, Brave, Halfling nimbleness, advantage/resistance to poison

FIGHTER ABILITIES: Protection, Second Wind

LANGUAGES: Common, Halfling

TOTAL HIT POINTS: 12

RACE	CLASS	PLAYER
Stout halfling	**Fighter**	**Journey**

XP POINTS	BG	ALIGNMENT
100	**Folk hero**	**Neutral Good**

STRENGTH	DEXTERITY	CONSTITUTION
15 (+2)	16 (+3)	14 (+3)

CHARISMA	WISDOM	INTELLIGENCE
7 (-2)	12 (+1)	13 (+1)

SAVING THROWS

STRENGTH: +4	CONSTITUTION: +5	WISDOM: +1
DEXTERITY: +3	INTELLIGENCE: +1	CHARISMA: -2

SKILLS

ACROBATICS:	0	INSIGHT:	+3	PERFORMANCE:	0
ANIMAL HANDLING:	+3	INTIMIDATION:	0	PERSUASION:	0
ARCANA:	0	INVESTIGATION:	0	RELIGION:	0
ATHLETICS :	+4	MEDICINE:	0	SLEIGHT OF HAND:	0
DECEPTION:	0	NATURE:	0	STEALTH:	0
HISTORY:	0	PERCEPTION:	0	SURVIVAL:	+3

ARMOUR CLASS	INITIATIVE	SPEED	PASSIVE PERCEPTION
16	+3	25 FT	11

EQUIPMENT & ATTACKS

Chain mail (AC 16), Short sword (1d6 piercing), buckler (AC +1), 2 handaxes (1d6 slashing), Explorer's pack, Artisan's pack

PROFICIENCIES

All armour and shields. Proficiency bonus +2 to simple weapons, martial weapons.

Meditation. Proficiency bonus +2.

SPELLS:

CANTRIPS:

FAVOURED ENEMY:

FAVOURED TERRAIN:

Demonica Scribe

LEVEL 1

Played by: **Rumour**

APPEARANCE: Spiral devil horns. Yellow demon eyes. Red complexion. Bad bitch attitude.

BACKSTORY: Demonica Scribe simply is. Her past is a secret. If you care to know more, you'll convince her to trust you.

TIEFLING TRAITS: Darkvision, resistance to fire, Thaumaturgy

LANGUAGES:
Common, Infernal, Elvish, Goblin

TOTAL HIT POINTS: 6

RACE	CLASS	PLAYER
tiefling	**wizard**	**Rumour**

XP POINTS	BG	ALIGNMENT
100	**acolyte (secret)**	**true neutral**

STRENGTH	DEXTERITY	CONSTITUTION
9 (-1)	11 (0)	11 (0)

CHARISMA	WISDOM	INTELLIGENCE
11 (0)	11 (0)	17 (+3)

SAVING THROWS

STRENGTH: **-1** CONSTITUTION: **0** WISDOM: **+2**
DEXTERITY: **0** INTELLIGENCE: **+5** CHARISMA: **0**

SKILLS

ACROBATICS:	0	INSIGHT:	0	PERFORMANCE:	0
ANIMAL HANDLING:	0	INTIMIDATION:	0	PERSUASION:	0
ARCANA:	+5	INVESTIGATION:	+5	RELIGION:	0
ATHLETICS :	0	MEDICINE:	0	SLEIGHT OF HAND:	0
DECEPTION:	0	NATURE:	0	STEALTH:	0
HISTORY:	0	PERCEPTION:	0	SURVIVAL:	0

ARMOUR CLASS	INITIATIVE	SPEED	PASSIVE PERCEPTION
10	0	30 FT	10

EQUIPMENT & ATTACKS

quarterstaff (1d6 bludgeoning), arcane focus, scholar's pack, spellbook

PROFICIENCIES

Proficiency bonus +2 to daggers, darts, slings, quarterstaffs, light crossbows

SPELLS: Burning Hands, Detect Magic, Disguise Self, Feather Fall, Magic Missile, Witch Bolt

CANTRIPS: Fire Bolt, Mending, Message

FAVOURED TERRAIN: Forests

FAVOURED ENEMY:

jace the bard!!! LEVEL 1

Played by: **Ian**

APPEARANCE: really cool popular ~~musicen~~ ~~mushishen~~ music player. he has long locs down to his butt and a smile handsum enuff to charm a bullywug! he is a ~~24~~ 25 year old MAN. he looks like me in 10 years i hope...

BACKSTORY: jace always wanted to be a bard ever since he picked up his dad's ~~guitar~~ lute. he's totally gonna be famous but for now he likes to play music for free and make friends with everyone because he's the nicest guy ever and everyone likes him!!!

1/2 ELF TRAITS: darkvishen, adv to charm, can't get put to sleep!

LANGUAGES: common, elvish, halfling

CHARACTER SHEET

TOTAL HIT POINTS: 9

RACE	CLASS	PLAYER
1/2 elf/ human	bard (duh)	ian

XP POINTS	BG	ALIGNMENT
100	entertaner	Lawful Good

STRENGTH	DEXTERITY	CONSTITUTION
9 (-1)	15 (+2)	12 (+1)

CHARISMA	WISDOM	INTELLIGENCE
16 (+3)	11 (0)	11 (0)

SAVING THROWS

STRENGTH: -1 CONSTITUTION: +1 WISDOM: 0
DEXTERITY: +4 INTELLIGENCE: 0 CHARISMA: +5

SKILLS

ACROBATICS:	+4	INSIGHT:	0	PERFORMANCE:	+5
ANIMAL HANDLING:	0	INTIMIDATION:	0	RELIGION:	0
ARCANA:	0	INVESTIGATION:	0	SLEIGHT OF HAND:	+4
ATHLETICS :	0	MEDICINE:	0	STEALTH:	0
DECEPTION:	0	NATURE:	0	SURVIVAL:	0
HISTORY:	0	PERCEPTION:	0		

ARMOUR CLASS	INITIATIVE	SPEED	PASSIVE PERCEPTION
13	+2	30 FT	10

EQUIPMENT & ATTACKS

1 LUTE!, lether armor (AC 11), dagger (1d4 piercing), r a p i e r (1d8 piercing), entertayner's pack

PROFICIENCIES

light armour, proficiency bonus = 2 to simple wepons, smol crossbows, so many swords

SPELLS: Charm Person, Disguys Self, THUNDERWAVE, Unseen Servant

CANTRIPS: Mage Hand, Friends

FAVOURED TERRAIN:

FAVOURED ENEMY:

Smashwell Stronk

LEVEL 1

Played by: <3 Greta Park <3

APPEARANCE: Quick of wit and thick with muscle, Smashwell is a huge, beefy, ripped, strong as heck giant woman (and fan of synonyms).

BACKSTORY: Smashwell loves reading more than anything in the world. Growing up in a culture dominated by, well, domination, this love caused more pain than joy. When it was clear her favourite activity was not some weird phase caused by human influence, her family made her choose between the written word or the clan. She chose.
Now she's a cleric, dedicated to healing instead of hurting. And she always has a good book.

HALF-ORC TRAITS: Dark vision, intimidation, relentless endurance, savage attack

LANGUAGES: Common, Orc, Elvish, Dwarven

TOTAL HIT POINTS: 9

RACE	CLASS	PLAYER
Half-orc	**Cleric**	**Greta**
XP POINTS	**BG**	**ALIGNMENT**
100	**Sage**	**Lawful Good**

STRENGTH	DEXTERITY	CONSTITUTION
13 (+1)	9 (-1)	12 (+1)
CHARISMA	**WISDOM**	**INTELLIGENCE**
7 (-2)	13 (+1)	10 (0)

SAVING THROWS

STRENGTH: +1 CONSTITUTION: +1 WISDOM: +3
DEXTERITY: -1 INTELLIGENCE: 0 CHARISMA: 0

SKILLS

ACROBATICS:	0	INSIGHT:	0	PERFORMANCE:	0
ANIMAL HANDLING:	0	INTIMIDATION:	0	PERSUASION:	0
ARCANA:	+2	INVESTIGATION:	0	RELIGION:	0
ATHLETICS:	0	MEDICINE:	+3	SLEIGHT OF HAND:	0
DECEPTION:	0	NATURE:	0	STEALTH:	0
HISTORY:	+2	PERCEPTION:	0	SURVIVAL:	0

ARMOUR CLASS	INITIATIVE	SPEED	PASSIVE PERCEPTION
10	-1	30 FT	11

EQUIPMENT & ATTACKS

mace (1d6 bludgeon), leather armour (AC 11), light crossbow and 20 bolts (1d6 pierce), a priest's pack, shield (AC +2), holy symbol—a novel

PROFICIENCIES

Meditation. Proficiency bonus +2

SPELLS: Wis. mod. + cleric level, clerics know ALL spells, must prep with meditation

CANTRIPS: Guidance, Spare the Dying, Thaumaturgy

FAVOURED ENEMY:

FAVOURED TERRAIN:

Ra'ven Tor'el

LEVEL 1

Played by: **Nathaniel Baron Medvedev**

APPEARANCE: Supernatural elven beauty. Long, luxurious black hair. A keen marksman's eye, emerald green. He has the less flashy, slim muscles of someone who actually uses them, unlike some vain bro-barian gym rat. Ra'ven Tor'el wears mostly plain travelling garb, his cloaks and tunics in the greens and browns of the forest.

BACKSTORY: Pride of the elven woodlands, Ra'ven Tor'el tragically lost both of his parents in a goblin attack, not unlike Batman. His cruel and cold lord uncle raised him, teaching him little about unconditional love but everything about being a ranger. On the eve of his sixteenth birthday, Ra'ven stole all he would need from his uncle and began his quest for revenge. He will find the goblins who orphaned him, or die trying.

LANGUAGES:
Common, Elvish, Dwarven

TOTAL HIT POINTS
12

RACE	CLASS	PLAYER
Wood Elf	**Ranger**	**Nathaniel**
XP POINTS	**BG**	**ALIGNMENT**
100	**Ranger**	**Lawful Good**

STRENGTH	DEXTERITY	CONSTITUTION
12 (+2)	16 (+3)	14 (+2)
CHARISMA	**WISDOM**	**INTELLIGENCE**
8 (-1)	15 (+2)	12 (+1)

SAVING THROWS

STRENGTH: **+4** CONSTITUTION: **+2** WISDOM: **+2**
DEXTERITY: **+5** INTELLIGENCE: **+1** CHARISMA: **-3**

SKILLS

ACROBATICS:	0	INSIGHT:	+4	PERFORMANCE:	0
ANIMAL HANDLING:	0	INTIMIDATION:	0	PERSUASION:	0
ARCANA:	0	INVESTIGATION:	+3	RELIGION:	0
ATHLETICS:	+4	MEDICINE:	0	SLEIGHT OF HAND:	0
DECEPTION:	0	NATURE:	+3	STEALTH:	0
HISTORY:	0	PERCEPTION:	0	SURVIVAL:	+4

ARMOUR CLASS	INITIATIVE	SPEED	PASSIVE PERCEPTION
14	+3	35FT	12

EQUIPMENT & ATTACKS

Leather armour (AC 11), 2 shortswords (1d6 piercing damage), Explorer's pack, Longbow and 20, arrows (1d8 piercing), Pan pipe

PROFICIENCIES

Light armour, medium armour, shields. Proficiency Bonus +2 to Simple weapons, martial weapons

SPELLS:

CANTRIPS:

FAVOURED ENEMY:
Goblins and hobgoblins

FAVOURED TERRAIN:
Forests